Promposal

Also by

Rhonda Helms

Never Too Late

Portrait of Us

Struck

(as Rhonda Stapleton)

Promposal

RHONDA HELMS

Simon Pulse

New York   London   Toronto   Sydney   New Delhi

SIMON PULSE

An imprint of Simon & Schuster Children's Publishing Division

1230 Avenue of the Americas, New York, New York 10020

This Simon Pulse edition February 2015

Text copyright © 2015 by Simon & Schuster, Inc.

Cover photograph of boy with balloons © 2015 by Getty Images/Paul Carrie

Cover photograph of field © 2015 by Thinkstock/klagyivik

All rights reserved, including the right of reproduction in whole or in part in any form.

SIMON PULSE and colophon are registered trademarks of Simon & Schuster, Inc.

For information about special discounts for bulk purchases, please contact

Simon & Schuster Special Sales at 1-866-506-1949 or business@simonandschuster.com.

The Simon & Schuster Speakers Bureau can bring authors to your live event. For more information

or to book an event contact the Simon & Schuster Speakers Bureau at 1-866-248-3049

or visit our website at www.simonspeakers.com.

Cover designed by Karina Granda

Interior designed by Tom Daly

The text of this book was set in Cantoria MT Std.

Manufactured in the United States of America

2 4 6 8 10 9 7 5 3 1

Library of Congress Cataloging-in-Publication Data

Helms, Rhonda.

Promposal / Rhonda Helms. — First Simon Pulse edition.

p. cm.

Summary: Camilla hopes her secret crush, Benjamin, might ask her to prom but feels pressured into accepting the invitation of a casual acquaintance, and Joshua has worked up the courage to ask his best friend, Ethan, to be his date when Ethan asks his help in crafting the perfect "promposal" for another boy.

[1. Dating (Social customs)—Fiction. 2. Proms—Fiction. 3. High school—Fiction.

4. Schools—Fiction. 5. Gays—Fiction.] I. Title.

PZ7.H375927Pro 2015   [Fic]—dc23   2014022769

ISBN 978-1-4814-2232-1 (hc)

ISBN 978-1-4814-2231-4 (pbk)

ISBN 978-1-4814-2233-8 (eBook)

To my daughter, Shelby, and my son, Bryan.

You both make me so proud.

Thanks for always making me giggle-snort.

CHAPTER ONE

Camilla

"Social norms are a challenging thing for us to face," Mrs. Brandwright said in a thoughtful tone. She paced up and down our classroom aisle, locking eyes with each of us for a moment. Her blond shoulder-length bob brushed her face as she walked. "So how have cultures evolved different perspectives on what is considered acceptable behavior in public? Because it does vary, depending on where you are."

I jotted the question down in my notebook, then went back to nibbling on my pen. I could pretty much predict that was going to be on our next pop quiz.

"I'm excited for us to start breaking these apart, to really *analyze* these norms, such as 'Don't talk too loud, or you'll bug people or look desperate for attention' or 'Control your emotions, or you'll appear volatile' or 'Stay outside of strangers' personal boundaries, or you'll be labeled creepy.'" She paused. "As a society, we learn that we must act a certain way around others, even from a young age. And as we get older, having internalized those rules, we grow uncomfortable when those around us break them. Who we perceive as rude or weird or lacking manners . . . or crazy." She locked her eyes on Carter, the guy behind me, who, from the sound of it, was halfway to snoozeville. *"Carter—wake up."*

He snorted and said in a bleary, sleep-filled voice, "I—I'm present."

The class tittered.

"Carter." Mrs. Brandwright gave that heavy teacher sigh. "I already took attendance. Pay attention, sir." She spun around and went back to the front of the classroom to write a few key terms about social norms on the chalkboard.

I turned my attention to my psychology notebook and tried to focus on her lecture, on writing notes. But once again my gaze slid, unbidden, to the back of Benjamin's neck. From my seat directly behind him, I could smell his light ocean-scented cologne wafting to my nose.

It was so, so hard not to lean forward and inhale.

Twelve freckles on the back of his neck. I knew because I'd counted them innumerable times since the beginning of the school year. Had stared in fascination at the small, dark blond swirl on the top of his head, which gave his hairline a twisty part and made the top spike in a haphazard fashion.

Benjamin ran a strong hand along his neckline, then scratched. Cheeks heated, I ripped my gaze away and fixed my attention on my notebook. Doodled a little in the margins, wrote my name in fancy script—*Camilla is super awesome.* It was stupid of me to spend all this time looking at him, I knew.

Not once since the school year began had the guy said more than five words to me in a row. Tests and papers were handed back in total silence. No chitchat before or after class. Hell, he barely even made eye contact with me. The last time it happened, I felt a strange zing through my whole body when those dark green eyes fixed on mine.

Then he'd looked away, back down to doodle in his notebook or sneak-read whatever novel was hidden in his lap, and I was reminded that Benjamin didn't give two shits about me. He probably didn't even know my name, despite the fact that I'd sat behind him since August. And given that it was already the beginning of April, I didn't see that changing anytime soon.

"Camilla," Mrs. Brandwright said, snapping me out of my thoughts, "what about you?"

Shit. I had no idea what we were talking about. "Um." I cleared my throat and narrowed my eyes at the board to see what she'd written. "I . . ."

The sigh she gave me closely resembled the ones she typically reserved for Carter. Her brown eyes creased as she shot me an irritated look. "I asked when was the last time you've been in a socially uncomfortable situation because of another person."

"Oh." My brain scrabbled for an answer, and I tried to ignore the huffs of impatience around me. "When I went to see a movie last month, the row my aunt and I chose was empty, and we sat in the middle. And then this older guy took the seat right beside me, despite there being plenty available elsewhere."

"I hate when that happens," Megan, the brunette in the seat beside mine, mumbled. "Why is it always guys who do that?"

"Interesting." Our teacher leaned back against her desk and crossed her arms over her ample chest. "Is it really always males who break these societal rules, especially regarding personal boundaries?"

"I think females break them too," Benjamin said in his low, husky tone. "But in different ways and maybe with different intents."

Intents. Yeah, like wanting to touch every lean line of his body, the way I ached to. I bet he was always having girls cuddle up a little too close to him. Had to get a bit old for him, being so ridiculously hot.

Okay, he wasn't hot in the typical sense. His nose was a little crooked, his lips a bit on the thin side. He was tall and kind of lanky. But there was something magnetic about those dark green eyes, the way he seemed like he could see right inside you. Saw past the facade and pierced to the truth, even with a brief glance.

Plus, he was well-read, unlike most guys in school who whined about having to do any reading outside of class. I didn't remember ever seeing Benjamin without a book in hand. All those classic titles he toted around—*War and Peace*, *The Count of Monte Cristo*, even *Jane Eyre*—gave me snippets of his personality, made me want to know more.

The first time I saw him freshman year, walking down the hallway with a couple of guys, I felt the impact of it long afterward. There was an intensity in his eyes that I'd never seen in anyone else's, and I wanted more. But we never had classes together, never shared a lunch break. My experiences were limited to fleeting glimpses during the occasional shuffle between classes.

So when I discovered on our first day of senior year that we were both in this psych class, I'd reveled in the realization that this was my big chance. And then had found out quickly that Benjamin wasn't much of a talker—not to me, not to anyone. But when he did talk in class to answer questions or offer thoughts, he was intelligent, albeit succinct.

Mrs. Brandwright peeked down at her watch. "Okay, everyone,

grab your journals. Today's entry is going to be about *your* most recent experience with someone breaking a societal norm in your presence. Sitting too close, talking too loud, doing something that made you uncomfortable because it broke those 'silent rules' of manners we all seem to adhere to. Analyze what made you so uncomfortable with the experience and also tell me how you reacted to it."

The sounds of pencils and pens scratching across paper filled the silence in the room. For a moment, I watched Benjamin scrawl in his notebook, his left hand sweeping across the page. He paused, tilted his head in thought, then wrote more.

What was he writing in there?

My heart squeezed in my chest. I dropped my gaze to my paper and wrote about my movie theater awkwardness. How I'd spent the rest of the movie leaning closer to my aunt Betsy, and how we'd exchanged whispers about the creeper beside me. Yet I hadn't moved away from the guy.

I paused. Why was that? Why had I been so hesitant to just get up and find another seat?

Maybe I didn't want to offend the guy in case he really wasn't that bad of a person, I wrote on my paper. *Or make a public disturbance that might disrupt others and thus make* me *the jerk. Sometimes I worry too much about looking impolite—I worry what others will think of me. That people will think I'm just a rude teen and write me and my feelings off because of it.*

I chewed on my pen as I reread what I wrote. Part of the reason for me being like this, so overly concerned with pleasing people, was my mom, who was a little . . . over the top, to say the least. And part of it had to do with the desire to be liked.

The final bell rang—school done, hooray! I shoved those

uncomfortable musings to the back of my head and gathered my belongings. People hustled down the aisle in an effort to get out of the classroom and head home. I filed behind everyone, last to leave, and made my way out of the room.

Then stopped dead in the door. Blinked.

The hallway was lined with dozens of students along the lockers, all staring at me in eerie silence, hands tucked behind their backs. To the right, in the middle of the hall, I saw Zach, a guy in my statistics class who wore a touch too much body spray and laughed loudly. His black hair was slicked back, and he had on a tuxedo that looked a little big on him.

He stepped toward me and gave me a curt nod. I saw his hands tremble, and he clenched them at his sides. "Hey, Camilla."

My heart gave a stuttering thud. I tugged the sleeves of my sweater over my hands. "Um. Hi, Zach?"

What the hell was going on here? Was this part of some strange social mores experiment from psych class that I'd missed because of not paying attention? I guess that was what I got for staring at Benjamin so often.

Students started whispering furiously as they stared at us. Then, just behind Zach, I saw a crew for a local news station. The college-age girl holding the camera had a shit-eating grin that took up nearly half her face, and beside her was a tall, polished brunette woman in a navy blue suit.

Oh God. Whatever this was, it was going to be on TV.

The camera's light hit me right in the eyes, and I blinked.

"Camilla," Zach said in a bellowing voice. "As I'm sure you know, we're nearing springtime. Our high school journey is about to end."

I barely smothered a snort at his overly formal tone; my brain wasn't quite accepting what was happening, and I didn't know yet how to react. "Yes, Zach. I kind of had an inkling about that."

He thrust his chin in the air. "You and I have been acquaintances for a while now, and today I wanted to ask you something important." He dropped down to one knee, looked to his left, and nodded, and soft classical music filled the hallways.

One by one, a number of the students along the lockers came up to me, and each handed me a red rose until my arms were overladen with flowers. A few of the girls winked at me or gave me whispered cheers of encouragement. The sickly sweet scent of roses filled the air.

My stomach knotted. Suddenly, I knew beyond a shadow of a doubt what was coming, and I had the strong impulse to drop the flowers, shove Zach away, and barrel down the hall.

Don't do it, I mentally begged him. *Don't ask me, please.*

Fear and horror and those damned social mores Mrs. Brandwright had just talked about paralyzed me in place. The smile on my face was pinched so tight it hurt. I scoured the hall, looking for someone who might help get me out of this situation.

I was met with swooning girls, snorting guys.

And Benjamin. Standing there, hands thrust in his jeans pockets, face inscrutable, just watching everything happen.

Wonderful.

"You are the most beautiful girl in school, maybe even in all of Ohio," Zach declared, his loud tone grabbing my attention. "And I'd like to ask you to please accompany me to the senior prom. As my date. With me." His cheeks burned bright red.

"Um." I swallowed. My hands shook; I gripped the flower

stems tighter. This wasn't how I'd envisioned my promposal happening. Not with a TV crew. Not with Zach looking overly awkward and uncomfortable as he tried to woo me.

Not with Benjamin sitting on the sidelines, a witness to the whole thing.

"Say yes," someone to my right whispered.

"Yes, yes, yes," another guy chanted.

Students around us began clapping, saying yes over and over again. The camera swept across the crowd, taking in the full scene, and then that bright light swirled back to me.

I sucked in a shaky breath. Released it. Looked down at Zach. My throat was squeezed so tight I wasn't sure I could speak; frustration mingled with disappointment in my gut. I bit my lip and simply nodded my reply, tried to blink back the tears that threatened to burn my eyes.

The hallways exploded with applause, and the newscaster turned to the camera and began speaking. Zach stood and stepped toward me, his eyes bright with joy.

"It's going to be great," he whispered. "I can't wait for the end of May."

The newscaster came over and thrust a mike in our faces. "So, Zachary," she said, "how did you come up with the idea for this . . . 'promposal'?" She beamed us a smile, her white teeth perfect and straight.

Zach talked for a few moments, but I didn't hear what he said. All I heard was the dull roar in my head. The heated words that battered my brain. I'd said yes to Zach, had agreed to be his date because I'd been peer-pressured into it. There was no way I could turn him down, not with all these people looking at us.

And with a friggin' TV crew on hand, for crying out loud.

No hadn't been an option for me.

"Camilla," the woman said, "so what do you think you'll wear? Will you two coordinate your outfits?"

I mumbled some generic response and tried my best to give her a smile, though it felt like my face was cracking apart. I just wanted to go home, curl up on my bed, and cry. I hadn't envisioned my promposal happening like this. Not with a guy I barely knew.

The woman turned her attention back to the camera to finish up her segment, and several girls came up to me.

"Oh my God, that was the most romantic thing I've ever seen in my life," one freshman said. She pressed her hand to her heart and practically swooned right there. "I hope *my* senior promposal will be that amazing. You are so, so lucky."

I gave a weak nod, and they scampered off.

The hallways cleared out. Zach walked over to the newscaster and gave her a kiss on the cheek. "Thanks, Mom."

Oh God. *Seriously?* His mom. I should have known.

She and her camerawoman packed up the gear and left too.

Zach turned toward me, self-congratulation evident in the warm flush of his cheeks, the glow in his eyes. "Well, I'd better get going."

"Yeah. Me too."

I guess my tone wasn't as upbeat as I tried to make it. His brow furrowed, and some of the sparkle left his eyes. "You *do* want to go with me, don't you?"

The weight of the roses was making my arms tired. I shifted them a bit and glanced away, guilt twisting in my chest. What did I say to that without sounding like a total jerk? Despite his proclamation, I barely knew the guy. I sat in statistics with him this year, and on the rare occasion, we shared the same lunch table.

But that look on his face when he'd asked me . . . that flare of hope in his eyes . . . He'd taken a lot of time to set this up.

I forced a smile to my face. Mom would be proud. "I'm sure it'll be a lot of fun." When in doubt, deflect.

He didn't seem to notice I hadn't answered his question. He smiled and squeezed my arm. "Get those flowers in water before they start to wilt." Then he leaned close to me and brushed a small kiss across my cheek. "I'll see you on Monday . . . *date*."

With that, Zach sauntered off with more than a little swagger, like a guy who always wore a tuxedo to school, and turned the corner out of sight.

I was left alone in the hall now. Stomach knotted. Head swirling with doubts. What did I do now? I was totally stuck going to prom with someone I didn't have any feelings for. The secret fantasy I'd had in my head of Benjamin asking me to prom was now dead and gone for good.

Yeah, I'd known it wouldn't happen, but the hope had still been there.

With a heavy sigh, I plodded to my locker and then headed outside. Maybe my bestie, Joshua, would have some advice for me. God knew I had no idea how I was going to dig myself out of this hole.

CHAPTER TWO

Joshua

My breath huffed out in small clouds as I walked down the sidewalk with Camilla, who filled me in on her promposal disaster.

"Boy, did you get yourself into it good," I said with a low chuckle as I eyed her. She squinted in mock consternation at me. "I'm impressed, actually. Somehow, drama always seems to find you." I dug my gloved hands deeper into my coat pockets. Early April in Ohio was still far too cold, despite spring coming soon. I was counting the days until warmer weather.

Camilla exhaled loudly and shifted the massive rose bouquet in her arms. Her backpack slipped, so I nudged the strap up her shoulder. "I know. And I can't back out now because then I'll look like a jerk after Zach went through all that trouble. He basically made it impossible for me to refuse him by asking me in front of God and country."

"Well, I can't wait to see you on TV tonight," I replied in a bright tone; the poor girl was so down in the dumps it was killing me. Camilla was never depressed like this, so I knew this situation was hitting her hard. "Who knew Zach was such a romantic? Or such a schemer? I kinda wish a tux-clad boy would ask *me* to prom—does he have a cousin or a hot brother?" I gave her a broad wink.

"Very funny." She elbowed me, but there was a hint of a smile on her face.

I wheezed and gripped my side. "Sorry. I know you're upset. Just trying to make you laugh."

A streak of bright purple hair flopped across her brow. Camilla's shade of the month—her blond base usually had at least one other color layered in. She turned big, sad eyes to me, and my heart tightened in sympathy for her. "I just wanted one dance with Benjamin at prom," she whispered. "Just one chance to show him why he should notice me." Her cheeks burned a bit pinker.

"Honey." I reached over and took the massive bundle of roses from her arms. She sighed in relief and stretched her arms. "Just because you're going with Zach doesn't mean you can't still get your man. This isn't the end. I promise."

"Yeah, I bet he would be *thrilled* to slow dance with me and Zach." Her tone was slightly sardonic as she gave a mirthless laugh. "Not to mention whatever lucky girl Benjamin takes to prom. Maybe we could double-date."

"Seriously, don't write him off so quickly. I know prom is out of the question, but that doesn't mean you can't still date the boy otherwise. We just need to step up your game. Come up with a plan to win him." My phone vibrated, and I dug it out of my pocket to glance at the screen.

Free to hang out tmrw night?

My heart slammed against my rib cage. Ethan. I whipped my glove off so I could reply. *You betcha! ;-)*

Camilla's soft laugh wrapped around the two of us. In a singsong voice, she said, "Speaking of getting your man . . . I bet I know who that was."

I rolled my eyes and crammed my phone back in my jeans. "You don't know shit."

"Ethan Dreyfuss, age eighteen, hottie senior at our school who looks amazing in tight jeans—"

"Okay, okay." I interrupted her with another eye roll. "Fine. I admit, you know some shit." Of course she did. We only spent an hour or two every damn day commiserating with each other about Ethan and Benjamin.

"When are you gonna get off your ass and ask him out?"

"When are you gonna get off *your* ass and ask Benjamin out?" I retorted.

We turned the corner and headed down the narrow side street where both our houses were, just a block apart.

Camilla shoved that wayward lock of purple-streaked hair back under her black knitted cap. Her thick knee-high boots crunched along the snow-crusted edges of the sidewalk. "It's . . . different."

"Sexist much? No, it's not."

"This isn't about gender, you douchebag, and you know it. The difference is, you have a chance with your boy, whereas I don't." She stopped and grabbed my arm. "Seriously, when are you going to tell him?"

I sighed and pressed the bundle of roses to my nose. Inhaled. Donned a big, fake smile and aimed the gesture right at her. "Tell him what, dear? That I've been madly in love with him since middle school and I've just been waiting for him to realize I'm the guy of his dreams?"

She narrowed her eyes. "Precisely."

"I will when you tell Mr. Hotpants that you've had a dirty crush on him since freshman year," I retorted.

She scrunched her lips. "Then I guess we're at an impasse."

I chuckled. "At least we have each other."

"Thank God for that. I'd go nuts without you." She threaded her hand through my free arm. The smile on her face was genuine.

Despite how much we busted each other's balls, there was never any doubt of support. I appreciated that, depended on it. If I texted Camilla at one in the morning that I needed to talk, she'd sneak over and watch action movies with me while we stuffed our faces with ice cream and popcorn and sorted out my issues.

We proceeded walking. When we hit her house, a two-story white colonial with a neat lawn, she took half the roses from me. "The rest are for you." She smiled and pressed a cool kiss to my cheek.

"Oh, you shouldn't have. If I were straight, I'd be all over you."

"I know. I'm hard to resist." She gave me a cheeky grin. "If you and Ethan hang out this weekend, I want *all* the dirty details." She paused, and her blue eyes grew serious. "But really, do think about what I said. You know he's worth the risk. And with prom right around the corner . . . Well, don't be like me and get yourself saddled with the wrong date."

On that depressing note, she spun around and headed into her house.

I gripped the bundle and made my way to my house on the next block. Poor Camilla. Despite my ribbing, I'd been more than a little shocked when she'd told me what had happened. I couldn't imagine how hard that had to be for her, forced to go to prom with some random guy who'd asked her out of the blue.

Maybe she was right. Maybe I should take the bull by the horns and get Ethan before someone else did. Even if I framed it as a date among friends. Surely he'd be down with that. I could bring the topic up tomorrow night. My stomach lurched in nervous excitement.

I swung a left onto my sidewalk. Old snow was still packed on the cement, up the two stairs to our front door. I needed to come out and shovel that—no doubt Dad, in the throes of drafting the newest novel in his thriller series, was drowning in words and had forgotten to even take a shower this morning.

I strolled through the front door, dropped my bag on the floor, and headed to the kitchen to find a vase for the roses. They really were pretty, despite the circumstances. I fluffed and arranged them as best as I could and put the bouquet in the center of the kitchen table.

"Dad, I'm home," I hollered, and ducked my head in the fridge. My stomach was grumbling. I'd forgotten to pack a lunch, so I dug into the leftover Chinese takeout container and chowed down without bothering to heat it up.

"Joshua," Dad called from his office, "want pizza for dinner tonight?"

I whipped the pantry open and checked out what we had left. "Um, how about I make something for us instead? There's still chicken in the freezer, I think."

"If you want, sure." I heard the soft clack of him typing on his laptop. "I just have to finish this chapter."

Famous last words. I probably wouldn't see him before dinner. And no doubt after cramming in food, he'd run back to his computer to fit in *juuust* another page or two. I chuckled, set the chicken out to thaw, and then settled down to do a bit of home-work.

Which lasted all of five minutes before I tugged my phone out and flipped through my photos. I hadn't seen Ethan today, since he'd had an impromptu Spanish tutoring session during lunch—our only shared time together this year.

I pulled up a picture of him I'd snapped earlier this week during lunch when he wasn't looking. Dark brown hair just a touch too long that swept across his brow. Gray eyes, thick lashes, the sexiest mouth, tilted at the corners as he laughed at something a guy at our table had said. Slender body with lean muscles honed from years of swim practice.

My throat tightened, and that familiar ache welled up in my chest. Ethan was the perfect guy. Friendly, enthusiastic, funny, athletic but not cocky. Hot as hell. Everyone loved him.

He and Camilla were my two best friends—the three of us had clicked back in middle school, when we'd been assigned to work together on a book report. The moment eleven-year-old Ethan had suggested we do our report on *Flowers in the Attic*, a book he'd snuck from his older sister and read, I knew I was gonna love him. Not to mention the fact that the three of us had spent more than one Saturday checking out and ranking hot guys at the mall.

"Joshua," Dad hollered from his office. "Which sounds scarier to you—being shoved in a tiny pitch-black room or in a metal-studded cage?"

"They both sound awful. But I think not being able to see would be worse. The fear of anticipation will get you every time."

"Yeah," he muttered. "That's true. Oh, maybe I can put the spiked cage *in* a pitch-black room. Yeah, that could really freak the girl out and make her talk." I heard his typing pick up again.

Dad had a disturbed mind. I still read all his books, though usually in a well-lit place and not near bedtime. Learned that lesson the hard way a few years ago.

My tabby cat, Milkshake, wandered up to the table and started rubbing her tiny gray head along my calf. I reached down and scratched her furry neck, and she purred in delight. Then I turned my attention back to the books. Shifted in my chair. Got up to crack open a fresh can of Dr Pepper from the fridge. Eyed my notes without really seeing them.

God, this was super boring. I shoved the material into my backpack. Eh, maybe homework tomorrow. Or more likely, Sunday night right before bed. I sipped my drink and then sent Ethan a text. *Whatcha doin?*

My phone buzzed a minute later. *Homework. :-P You?*

Attempting it. Blech. So what are we doin tmrw night?

It's a surprise. Be ready at 5.

Tingles swept across my skin. Ethan was unpredictable, to say the least. I could only venture a guess on what he was planning. Maybe an outing somewhere fun or a cool new coffee shop he'd discovered.

My phone buzzed again; another message from him. *Looking forward to talking to you—have important Q to ask.*

With that, my heart skipped a beat or two, then began a furious gallop in my chest. A big question? What could it be?

Surely it wasn't . . .

No. Don't go down that road, I chided myself. Just because Camilla got asked to prom didn't mean Ethan was going to ask me. Our friendship was solid—okay, his side was solid, while mine was smoldering with unrequited love—but there hadn't been any indicators Ethan was into me that way. To my eternal sadness.

Then again, Camilla's promposal had come out of the blue. It did happen sometimes. Why couldn't it happen for me?

Whatever it was, it was probably important. Ethan wasn't one to mince words. My hands shook, and I fumbled the letters but managed to type out *I'll be ready.*

And if he didn't ask me, I would take the chance and ask him—fate was giving me an opportunity I couldn't let go. I put my phone on the table and tried to focus on homework. But all I could think about was him.

CHAPTER THREE

Camilla

I hope you appreciate how hard I'm working," I said to my mom as I put the last of the pasta in the pantry. "These shelves were heinous."

"Well, you are a good girl, and you listen to your mama," she replied from her crouched position on the floor in front of the fridge. I could hear her huffing, the rhythmic sweeps of her scrubbing the interior.

Saturday mornings and early afternoons were made for cleaning, according to my mom. Sadly, I disagreed and felt that time was much better for sleeping or giving in to my rare bouts of lazy time, but I wasn't in any position to argue with her. Over the years I learned if I did a burst of activity for an hour or two, she usually backed off enough so I could spend the rest of my weekend how I wanted.

Mom started singing an old Romanian song, and I found myself humming along. It was one she'd brought with her from the "old country" when she moved to the United States as a teenager with her parents and younger brother, my uncle Andre. Mom still had an accent, despite having lived here for so long, and when she got in a pissy mood, she'd speak a flurry of Romanian to me.

Not that I always understood what she was saying, of course. Dad, who was American, only spoke English, so that was our main language in the house.

"—college," Mom was saying.

I snapped my attention back to her. "Um, what?"

She slit her eyes as she peered at me. "We need to pick which college you are going to attend. Time is running out to accept the offers."

"I know, I know." Technically, we had until early May to accept, but Mom had been hounding me every week since December to choose which school I was going to start in the fall. I'd gotten accepted into three different colleges, but I was torn about which one would be right for me.

There was a good state school twenty minutes from our house that had a great K–12 education program so I could follow my dream of becoming a history teacher. The second school was in southern Ohio, about three and a half hours away. And the third was in Chicago.

"Well, we are all waiting on you," she said. "I don't understand what is taking so long. It's not like you are picking a husband or anything."

I turned my attention back to the pantry and rolled my eyes. Her pushiness made me want to choose Chicago, which was a good seven-hour drive away from home. "I promise you won't have to wait much longer."

"Where is Joshua going to go? Did he decide yet?"

"Columbia University in New York City told him a couple of weeks ago that he got in." I chuckled. "And that was the end of the search for him." When Joshua had gotten his acceptance letter, he'd legit started tearing up in excitement. We'd both danced around his house for a full ten minutes. Doing music *and* living in NYC for four years? A total win-win.

Though it was going to be so, so hard to be that far from my best friend.

"I'm glad to hear it." *Scrub, scrub.* "Your father won't be home until this evening. One of his employees called in sick, so he's working late."

"That's too bad. Maybe I can run him up some dinner later."

"You are a good girl." I heard the smile in my mother's voice. "He would appreciate it, I am sure."

My dad owned a small but thriving jewelry store in a bustling strip plaza. Five years ago, he'd declared to me and Mom that he was quitting his job at an accounting firm to start his own company. I'd assumed Mom would have a stroke when he told her, but she'd stayed surprisingly calm and told him she would support him in this. We both had seen far too many nights when Dad would come home tired and miserable.

Now he was still tired, but I'd never seen him happier. My parents had stopped fighting as much, even. Crazy how taking a risk and following your dreams led to happiness all around.

I straightened up the pantry a bit more, stalling. I knew Mom was going to tell me to tackle the bathroom next, and I *so* did not feel like scrubbing toilets. As I pondered how to get out of the task today, the doorbell rang.

"Will you get that, please?" Mom asked.

I glanced down at my clothes with a wrinkle of my nose. Stained sweatpants and a beat-up T-shirt. "But I look like ass."

She whipped her head around to eye me with a stern glare, and I instantly regretted the cuss word. "Language, miss."

"Sorry," I said in a soothing tone. "That slipped out."

The doorbell rang again.

Her eyebrow rose.

With a sigh, I clomped my way to the door and whipped it open. There stood Zach, a broad grin on his face.

"Hey," he said.

My eyes widened, and it was so hard not to just slam the door in his face and run to my room to change. Despite my mom's huff of displeasure at my word choice, I *did* look like ass. In general, I preferred that people at school not see me in a state of assiness. Even Joshua knew better than to come over until later in the afternoon on Saturdays. "Um. Sorry. I'm in the middle of cleaning," I said with an apologetic wave of my hand over my outfit.

His gaze raked my form, and it didn't seem like he cared what I was wearing. "No biggie. Need help?"

"Who is at the door?" my mom asked loudly. She couldn't see us from her spot in the kitchen.

Zach peered over my shoulder.

"It's a friend, Mom." I squeezed the door a bit closer around me. "Thanks, but I'm good. Did . . . you need something?"

He cleared his throat, and a gust of brisk wind whipped his hair around. His cheeks pinkened, and goose bumps broke out on my flesh from the chilly air. "I came to talk about prom with you," he said in a low voice.

It hadn't even been twenty-four hours since he'd asked me. He already wanted to start talking about it? I'd barely accepted the fact that I'd said yes.

"Invite your friend in, Camilla," Mom hollered. "What are you, being rude? Leaving her standing in this cold weather?"

It was hard to dampen down the sudden swell of irritation. "Please, come inside." I opened the door wider and let him in.

He sighed in relief when he stepped in, then looked around the room. Stripped his coat off and held it out to me to hang up. *Make yourself at home, why don't you.* "Your place is great."

I hung his coat up. "Can I get you something to drink?" See, even pissed off, I could remember my manners.

"What do you have?"

Mom walked into the living room and stopped. "Oh, it is a boy, not a girl." She swatted my arm, then fluffed her hair and smoothed the front of her shirt and pants. "Why didn't you tell me you had a male guest?" By the hungry gleam in her eye, I could tell she was already planning our wedding.

Zach thrust out his hand to her. "Hello. I'm Zach. I go to school with Camilla."

"Yes, he and I are in statistics together," I interjected. I was so not ready for Mom to find out we were prom dates. Because, to be honest, part of my brain had been scrabbling since yesterday for ideas on how to get out of going with him. Which sounded awful, I knew, but I couldn't help it.

"Are you hungry?" Mom grabbed his arm and sat him down on the couch. Her smile was so big that she looked almost crazy. "Would you like a sandwich? Or I can make you some chicken or—"

"Mom," I said as I shot her a look.

I knew why she was so excited about Zach being here. I never had guys over, ever. Well, except Joshua, but she'd stopped trying to matchmake us in seventh grade when we finally told her he was gay. Though she did try to point out attractive guys to the two of us when we were out in public.

"I'm good on food, thank you," Zach said. "But . . . maybe a soda?"

With a quick nod, she ran into the kitchen.

I sat on the chair opposite the couch. "I'm sorry," I said with an awkward laugh. "She doesn't get out of the house much."

"That is not true," Mom called from the kitchen. "I have book club and movie club *and* wine club."

I gave a real laugh this time. "Okay, her social life is better than mine, if I'm honest." After clearing my throat, I rested my clenched hands in my lap. I knew my discomfort had to be radiating from me, because my back was one big knot of tension, but Zach didn't seem to notice. He just stared at me with a blasé expression.

Mom gave him the drink, then stood behind the couch, eyeing us closely.

"Thanks," I told her.

Awkward silence.

"Well. I guess I will leave you two to talk." She shuffled back into the kitchen, and I heard the scrubbing start again.

"Um. So. What did you need to see me about?" I asked him.

He took a sip of his drink, then put it on the coffee table. Twisted the cuff of his sweater. Sipped again. Was he nervous? "Well, I was talking to my mom—"

"The newscaster." Boy, had the woman looked excited in her segment last night. I'd watched it up in my room. Thankfully, it had been the ten o'clock news, and my mom and dad had already been sawing logs in bed. So they'd missed the hubbub, hadn't seen my beet-red face and painful smile as I agreed to go to prom with Zach. Though it seemed like half the school had seen the segment and had blown up my phone and Facebook page with messages about it last night and this morning.

"Yeah. She said we should get working early on coordinating our outfits. Picking what colors we want, where we should go to dinner, and so on. She found your address and suggested I drop by."

"I see." I dropped my gaze to where my fingers picked at the hem of my T-shirt. "I wasn't quite prepared to start talking about this yet," I admitted. I sucked in a steadying breath. Maybe now that we were alone, I could tell him I wasn't so crazy about being his date. Tell him that it was one thing to do a big promposal like that when you and the person were dating. Or at least knew more about each other than first and last names.

"What do you think about blue?" he continued. "We could do light or dark. Or maybe a nice royal blue."

God, was he not even listening to me? I glanced up at him, a few frustrated words on the tip of my tongue, and saw the excitement in his eyes, the sweet smile on his face as his eyes met mine. My gut pinched, and the anger fell away.

No, I didn't have any feelings for this guy. No attraction whatsoever. But that didn't mean we couldn't go as friends, right? Maybe I should use this time to get to know him instead of letting bitter disappointment sour the rest of my senior year.

Benjamin was a pipe dream, that ungettable get so far out of the realm of possibility that he wasn't real. But I could attempt to build a friendship with Zach so we would at least somewhat enjoy prom together.

"Blue's not bad, but I really like red," I finally said.

I saw the moment the tension leaked out of his body. He nodded. "Yeah. Red's nice too."

I grabbed a sheet of paper off the side table, ripped a corner off, and scribbled my cell phone number down. "I really don't mean to be rude, but I have a bunch of chores I have to finish today. Can we talk about this sometime next week?"

He glanced down at the number, then stuffed it in his pocket and stood. "That'd be great. Sure. No problem."

After getting his coat, I walked him to the door. He gave me a quick nod and headed outside. I closed the door behind him, shivering with the slip of brisk wind that snuck in. Then I leaned my back against the slab of wood and sighed. This wasn't how I'd envisioned things going, but I could work with it. Or at least give it a damn good try.

And maybe if I kept telling myself that, I'd finally start to feel it.

The house was silent. Too silent.

Mom crept into the living room. The grin on her face was so big that I knew she'd overheard. "Oh, my baby!" she said as she clapped her hands to her chest. "You have your date to prom! And we have so much planning to do. But we really should talk about red—I don't find it flattering for your skin."

"Mom," I started, but she kept talking.

"I'm going to call your aunt," she continued. "She will help us find the perfect fabric."

"Mom."

"We can start looking tonight. No, tomorrow night. I think she is busy with something at church."

"Mom!" I waved my hands in front of her face. "I know you're excited, but he and I are just friends." Kinda. "This isn't a real date. So don't start looking for a wedding dress or anything."

"Wedding dress?" Mom scoffed and rolled her eyes. "Don't be ridiculous, Camilla. Now you are just talking silly." She pranced into the kitchen, and a moment later I heard her talking in a quick rush. Probably already on the phone with Uncle Andre's wife, Betsy, who was a part-time seamstress. The conversation was punctuated with excited squeals and a ten-minute analysis of which fabric would be best to use for crafting my dress.

Look on the bright side, I told myself as I trudged upstairs to shower and change. At least I got her off my back about chores.

CHAPTER FOUR

Joshua

I stared down the lane and made sure my foot was behind the line. Drew my arm back and flung the ball. It flew straight across the smooth wood at first, then curved toward the right gutter.

"No!" I cried out as the ball took out only the very last pin. I spun around and faced Ethan, who was sitting on the plush dark purple seat behind the score stand. "Well, it's official. Nothing about me is straight."

He smirked. "We wouldn't want you any other way." He glanced down at the scores. "Joshua Mendez, seventy-six. Ethan Dreyfuss, ninety-five. Still pretty close, and we're not done yet."

"Much closer than their game," I noted with a nod to the lane on our left. For the last half hour, Ethan and I had been observing the couple—who appeared to be on a first date—to see what would happen after the woman had proclaimed to the guy with a flirty flush that she'd never been bowling. The man, though, had apparently missed all her signals. Instead of helping her, he was too busy trying to show off his prowess with a bowling score that tromped hers into the dust.

Ethan shook his head. "He's gonna blow it if he doesn't rein it in some." The woman was already showing signs of frustration, and her stiff body language was screaming that the date would end early. Too bad the guy was blind.

"Five bucks says she leaves in the next half hour."

One eyebrow raised, Ethan stuck his hand out. "You're on." When our palms connected, I felt a warm shiver travel up my arm. One touch wasn't enough. I wanted to slide my thumb across the top of his hand, but I couldn't.

I withdrew my hand. Bit my lip and sat down to watch Ethan, who was up next. I hadn't expected tonight's surprise to be bowling, but I had to admit, I was having fun. Then again, he and I could write a grocery list and make it fun.

Ethan bent over just a touch, and his skinny jeans tightened over his ass. I turned my gaze away, looked at the scoreboard. The couple beside us. The family on the other side. Anything to help me dim this heated flush sweeping through my veins.

Ethan hadn't yet asked me whatever it was he was going to ask, and it didn't seem right to bring up prom in the middle of the bowling alley. So I tried to just push aside that little bubble of anxious excitement and focus on the here and now. Spending time with my other best friend. That bittersweet tinge in my heart grew larger when Ethan spun around and raised his fists in the air.

"Yes!" he cried out. "I got a strike—first one of the night!" He looked thrilled and proud of himself, his eyes glowing, grin wide.

I stood and gave him a high five. "Nice job."

As he passed I smelled his familiar rich cologne, and I closed my eyes for just a moment. Breathed. My mouth dried up. I fumbled for my ball and peeked over at the couple on our left.

The woman stood at the line while the man held her ball and was trying to show her the proper way to throw.

"He's messing it up," Ethan said in my right ear, and I jumped at the sensation of his warm breath caressing my skin. "He should be right behind her while she holds the ball, making every excuse he can to touch her. This date should be about her, not about bowling."

He was right. For the tiniest of seconds, I pretended this was a real date with Ethan. That when I went up to the line, he'd stand behind me, grab my wrist, and slowly show me the correct way to throw the ball. The muscles of his strong torso would be pressed to my back.

I swallowed. Kept my attention focused on the couple. The woman threw the ball, which went right into the gutter. She said something to the guy in a low voice. He responded, waving his hands. She gave him a polite, strained smile, then sat down and began to remove her shoes.

"I won," I said quietly, though there wasn't any victory in it. Now I just felt bad—it wasn't a game for her, and the guy looked irritated at his bowling night being disrupted before it was over.

Ethan pressed a fiver in my hand. "That sucks. Wish we could buy her a beer. She looks like she could use it."

She grabbed her purse and the rental shoes and walked away, with the guy staring dumbly at her retreating figure.

"God, some people can't see what's right in front of them," Ethan said as he plopped into the seat.

Oh, irony. Thy name is Ethan. I barely held in my sudden laughter. "Yeah. Totally." If only he knew. I turned my attention back to the lane and threw my ball. "Knocked down five that time."

"See?" Ethan said with an encouraging grin. "You're already getting better."

We finished our round—Ethan won by sixteen points—and grabbed a couple of slices of pizza. The silence was comfortable for several minutes, and we watched others bowl.

"This place is hopping on a Saturday," Ethan remarked. His lean fingers stroked the edge of his napkin.

"Mm-hmm," I said as I finished my last bite. Now that the game was over, I was back to thinking about *the Question*, wondering what the hell Ethan had to ask that was so important.

And I couldn't stop mulling over the best way to take the bull by the horns and ask Ethan if he'd go with me to prom. Despite spending most of yesterday and today thinking about it, I wasn't quite sure how to approach the subject without sounding dumb or desperate. Should I wait until he brought it up? Or just outright ask him if he was planning to go?

Though I already knew he was. We'd talked about it earlier this year with Camilla, in fact.

Anxiety twisted my gut, and I wished I hadn't eaten all that pizza. I dropped my hands to my lap and gathered my courage. "Hey. So . . . you said you wanted to talk."

A flicker of emotion I didn't recognize flitted across his face. "Oh. Yes." He wiped his fingers on the napkin and drew in a deep breath. A light pink flush stole across his cheeks and heightened his skin's contrast with his dark strands of hair. "I . . . was hoping we could go somewhere a little more private. You ready to head out of here?"

My heart was beating so irregularly now I was afraid I might pass out. Ethan looked nervous too. Perhaps I might not have to ask him after all. "Sure. Yeah. I'm all done. Yeah, let's go."

We stood and dumped our trash, returned the rented shoes, and donned our coats and hats. My hands shook so badly it took me a couple of tries to get the zipper right. Luckily, Ethan didn't notice. I tucked my scarf around my neck and we headed out into the brisk, dark night.

The bowling alley was only a few blocks away from our neighborhood, but given the chill in the night air, we'd taken Ethan's car. I hopped into the passenger seat and we sat in the spot for a few minutes while the car warmed up. My brain was screaming at Ethan in desperation for him to speak *now, now, now*, but I tried to hold myself in check. No sense pushing him—I knew Ethan would talk when he was ready. He wasn't a blurting type of guy. Not like me.

Finally, when warm air blasted through the vents, Ethan pulled out of the spot and we headed down the road. An instrumental song that sounded like it was from the 1920s filled the car.

"Still hot for Gatsby, huh?" I teased. Last year we'd read *The Great Gatsby* in English and then watched the recently remade movie. For weeks after, Ethan had gone around calling me and Camilla "old sport." By week four, she was ready to choke him.

"You have to admit, that book was amazing." He sighed and turned up the music a touch. "Imagine if we could have lived back then. The decadent parties. And that music . . ." He turned onto the main road, driving through our local Metroparks. We whipped past snow-covered trees until he turned into a parking spot for our favorite sledding hill.

I jumped out of the car and stared down the steep decline. Ethan got out as well, and the breeze played with his hair. With the soft golden glow of the streetlight illuminating his face, he seemed angelic. I bit back a desperate sigh.

God, just once . . . just one time in my life, I'd like to have him look at me like he had feelings for me too.

"Check the trunk," Ethan said. There was a light twinkle in his eyes as he used the key to unlock it.

Inside were two sleek black sleds.

I laughed, my face nearly splitting in two with a wide grin. "Really?"

"Why not?" He shrugged. "Been a while since we've gone sledding."

Back in middle school, he, Camilla, and I had spent hours outside, sliding down and trudging up this very hill. Laughing and sledding until we were practically numb. Then making our way through the thick snow to his house, where his mom had hot cocoa waiting for us.

"Okay, you're on." I grabbed the sleds and handed him one, and we crunched through the icy snow to the very edge of the hill. I laughed as I eased myself onto the sled. Glanced over at Ethan, who shot me a cocky look. "Five bucks say I make it to the bottom before you."

"Oh, that deal is on. I want my money back." He slit his eyes in determination, then faced forward.

"Three . . . two . . . one!"

We took off in a rush. Cold air smacked my face, ripped through my sinuses as I plunged down the hill. Ethan whooped and we soared, nearly neck and neck.

I hit a bump and almost flipped over. "Holy shit!" I called with a laugh, gripping the sides of the sled tighter. My heart galloped.

He edged out in front of me and made it to the bottom just a second before I did. His sled toppled over, and he burst into riotous laughter. "Oh my God. That was more amazing than I remembered. Why did we stop doing this?"

I lay back in the sled and stared at the smattering of stars peeking through the trees around us, my cheeks burning from the wind and from my smiling muscles. My heart was still racing, and I felt so alive. "I have no idea. But we should do it again."

"Okay. But before we do . . ." Ethan sat up, and I could feel the weight of his stare on me.

With his words, my lungs squeezed to the size of grapes, and I sat up as well. Tucked my hands in my lap and let my booted feet dangle off the edge of the sled. "Yes?"

"I . . ." Ethan cleared his throat, peeked at the sky. "I needed to talk to you about prom."

OhGodohGodohGod. I couldn't tear my gaze away from his dimly lit profile. The cold faded away. Tendrils of anticipation wrapped around my chest, tightened.

Here it comes.

"There's . . . someone at school I want to ask to prom, but I don't know how," he said in a rush. "So I was hoping you could help me since you're so talented and smart." He looked at me, and his eyes bore a strange vulnerability I'd never seen in them before.

My stomach fell as his words pierced my frantic brain, and all the air whooshed out of my lungs.

Ethan wanted my help asking another guy to prom. I didn't even know he liked someone. Crushing disappointment settled over me like fine snowflakes and froze my warm, hazy glow.

"Ah. I see. Who's the lucky fellow?" It was hard to keep my voice steady and light.

"Noah McIntyre." Ethan exhaled, and a puff of steamy air floated between us. He shot me a wry grin. "He's in biology with me—oh, and he's the lead in *Oklahoma!* And I don't know what to do so he'll say yes."

My mind flashed an image of a tall blond with bright green eyes. I knew who he was talking about now. A transfer student who came to our school his junior year from California. Gorgeous, witty, perfect abs. I think he was even nominated for homecoming king back in October, despite still being relatively new.

I stood and picked up the sled, my limbs weighing a thousand pounds each. What an idiot I was, thinking even for a second that Ethan might have brought me out here to ask me to prom. Of course he wanted me to help him ask someone else. Because that was my luck.

Thank God I hadn't yet asked him to go with me. Having him say no would have crushed me beyond repair.

"Why not just go up to him and ask him to prom?" I asked, my tone a bit flat.

He stood too, moved closer. He was only a couple of inches taller than me, but at the moment I felt a lot smaller. "Because I want it to be just right. And I know that if anyone can help me, it's you. You're the only one I trust." He reached his free hand out and took mine, but I barely felt it. "Please."

"Why Noah?" I said, because it appeared I had some dark desire to torture myself. As if the answer wasn't obvious.

Ethan's face softened, and his lips curved into a secret smile. He chewed on his bottom lip. "I just . . . I really like him. And I think he likes me too. Sometimes our eyes connect in class, and there's this zing there."

The hint of need in his face brought a surge of guilt-mingled pain to my heart. Ethan didn't know I loved him, despite my internal agony. How could he know? All these years, I'd never let anything on, had been so careful to keep my romantic feelings from him so as not to pressure him. All this waiting-for-the-right-time crap had now bitten me in the ass. It wasn't his fault I'd built up some stupid expectation, some delirious hope that one day we might end up together.

I knew my friend needed me, and I also knew I couldn't let him down.

But I couldn't deny the nut-kicking realization that a relationship really wasn't going to happen with him, ever. We'd settled too deeply into the friend zone for me to dig my way out. Reality was hitting me hard upside the head right now.

Yeah, I got it, universe. Loud and clear.

I released his hand and rubbed my nose, which was beginning to freeze. Tried to avoid the pleading look in his eyes. "Okay, sure. I'll help." What else could I say? *No, because I was hoping you and I would go instead?*

"You. Are. A. God," he said, relief clear on his face. "I know you'll help me make this the most amazing event ever." Ethan dropped his sled and wrapped me in his arms, and it was almost impossible for me not to breathe his shampoo, the warmth of his skin, deeply in. "Thank you. *Thank you.*"

I let my sled go too and gave him an awkward pat on the back, then moved away. "What are friends for?"

RHONDA HELMS

An hour later, I was sitting on my couch, a blanket tucked around me, watching some weird, random black-and-white murder mystery on TV. My phone was on the coffee table; I saw it buzz and light up, but I didn't move for it.

Right now, I just needed to nurse my wounds. Figure out how to piece my pathetic broken heart back together. All I had to do was get over Ethan by Monday, then help him win the guy of his dreams so they could enjoy their romantic prom together.

Piece of cake. I snorted.

Speaking of dessert . . . I hopped up and headed to the fridge. Surprisingly, Dad had gone to the grocery store while I was out, and he'd gotten us some ice cream. Yeah, it was cold, but come on. Rocky road ice cream. Like I was going to pass that up.

I made a huge, heaping bowl and settled back into my seat. Checked my phone.

I hope your day is going better than mine. :-P Whatcha doin? How was your eve w/ Ethan?

I typed Camilla a response. *Eating ice cream and watching a shitty movie.* She was smart enough to read between the lines.

Her reply dinged a minute later. *Nuff said. On my way. Will bring chips and Legolas.*

She totally got me. That made me grin. I couldn't count how many marathons of *The Lord of the Rings* trilogy she and I had done over the last few years, if only because we loved to watch Orlando Bloom run around and look hot.

Perfect, I texted back. *Rocky road awaits you.*

CHAPTER FIVE

Camilla

O w!" I cried out after an elbow clipped my side.

"Oh. Sorry," some huge guy said as he kept barreling down the crowded hallway.

I grumbled under my breath as I rubbed my sore rib cage. Yeah, it was shaping up to be a real Monday, all right. I'd left my packed lunch on the kitchen counter this morning and didn't have any cash on me, so my stomach was grumbling like crazy with hunger. I'd bombed my French test. People all day had asked me what it felt like to be a celebrity on the news. Zach had already sent me half a dozen texts asking me how I was and if I wanted to hang out one day after school this week.

And now my rib was throbbing like mad.

A light touch on my elbow snapped my attention up.

"You okay? I saw what that meathead did. That had to hurt." Noah McIntyre gave me a warm smile of concern.

I frowned, torn between appreciation for his concern and solidarity for Joshua's personal agony over the drama Noah was unknowingly causing. "Oh. Um, yeah. Thanks for asking."

His eyes twinkled; the green color perfectly matched the scarf draped over his shoulders. "Maybe bring some armor tomorrow. It's a war zone in here." With that, he sauntered off toward his class.

I huffed a sigh and dug my phone out of my pocket. I wanted to be angry with Noah, demand he stop being that damned attractive so Ethan would stop noticing him, but I knew that would be ridiculous. Not to mention the fact that he really was a nice guy.

I shot Joshua a text as I strolled along the edge of the hallway. *Making it thru the day ok?* Saturday night, we'd stayed up well past midnight, whining and eating way too much ice cream.

My phone vibrated. I opened it and saw a picture of Joshua's face, his eyes sad and mouth exaggerated in a deep frown. His text underneath said, *I'm dying on the inside. But at least my hair looks great.*

I couldn't help but laugh. *That's right. Keep your dignity—& tell me what product you're using to get that fab volume.*

Another picture, this time with him giving me a brave smile.

Hang in there, I replied. *We'll figure this out together, I promise. For now, just tread H2O.*

I stuck my phone in my pocket so I wouldn't get busted by a teacher and sucked in a deep, steadying breath. My heart thrummed beneath my rib cage. Psychology. Time to see Benjamin.

The phone buzzed again.

Okay. You busy Friday evening?

I groaned. After Zach's texts this morning asking me out, I'd explained I was busy with homework after school this week, hoping he'd take the hint and give me some breathing room. So much for the gentle approach.

I'll let you know, I replied, then stuck the phone in my purse so I wouldn't feel him reply.

I clutched my book and notebook closer to my torso and stepped into the room. As had happened with every class today, I got a bunch of people buzzing to me about Friday's promposal. *Last class of the day,* I told myself. I just needed to get through the rest of today and then I could go home, and people would stop talking about it.

"You looked great on TV!" Janie, a cheerleader, told me.

"Thanks." I smiled and headed toward my desk. Carter, hoodied head down on his desk, was already asleep behind me, and Benjamin had his notebook open and was writing something.

At least I could count on the two of them. For once, I was looking forward to Benjamin's typical silence. I'd had enough public attention for a lifetime.

Mrs. Brandwright stood from behind her desk. "Okay, let's get started. We have a lot of lecture to cover, and then for the last half of class we have another special project to start."

That got some excitement going. People stirred in their seats and began whispering. Mrs. Brandwright's class projects were usually fun and strange. Last semester, we discussed parenting and were assigned baby dolls we had to carry around with us for a week. One guy had kept his nestled under his shirt the whole time, like he was pregnant.

Mrs. Brandwright began her furious scrawl across the chalkboard while talking in a fast clip, and the class quieted down as we began writing notes. I was too busy to even look at Benjamin. Well, not more than once or twice, anyway.

There was a startling tap on my left knee, the side against the wall. I peeked down and saw Benjamin's left arm dropped to his side, his hand touching my kneecap.

My heart gave a strange thud as I dropped my left arm. My fingers brushed his and I took the small note folded in his hand. He ducked his head back down and continued writing in his notebook.

I couldn't stop the slight tremor in my hand. What was Benjamin passing me a note about? Anticipation bubbled in my chest, and I forced myself to unfold the note slowly so Mrs. Brandwright wouldn't notice.

His writing was lean and strong, confident. The page only had one line of text with four words.

Saw you on TV.

I stared at the brief note for a good minute, wondering what to reply. This was so unexpected that my brain was pretty much useless right now. I swallowed, forced my brain to focus.

Write something clever, I ordered myself.

You and the rest of the school, hah, I added below his line.

Really witty, Camilla. But in my defense, he didn't give me much to work with.

I folded it back up and tried to hunch in my seat so I could tap his elbow. He dropped his arm, and I pressed the note into his fingers; my skin shivered in delight when our bare flesh touched again.

In a couple of minutes, I saw his left arm drop once more. I reached down and took the note from him, still unable to believe that I was actually passing notes with Benjamin, of all people. What planet was this? And even more ironic, I had the promposal to thank—Zach, specifically.

I opened the paper . . .

. . . and saw a doodle, similar in style to the ones that filled his notebook pages. It was an old-fashioned TV and in the middle of the screen was a rough sketch of my face in profile, but it was unmistakably me—my wavy hair, the slope of my nose, my lips. Coming off the top of my head and over the TV was an empty thought bubble.

I swallowed. Obviously a reference to my TV appearance. And he wanted me to fill in the thought bubble; that much was clear. But what should I write?

"Okay," Mrs. Brandwright interrupted my pondering. "Time for fun."

I sighed and tucked the note away. Well, at least I'd have time to chew on the perfect response. To write something that would keep the lines of conversation open with Benjamin. Despite the brevity of the note's text, this was the most we'd talked, well, ever. And he'd surprised me with that picture of me.

Surprised and flattered me. I was tempted to open it and stare at it, but I knew I'd get busted.

The class tucked away their books, and I did the same. We sat quietly as Mrs. Brandwright moved to the front of her desk and leaned against the edge.

"So, we've been talking about social mores. About how difficult it is to break out of them, how it pushes our comfort zones. We retreat into the safety of 'manners' because we don't want to offend." She paused, and her eyes had an excited gleam. "Well, we're about to challenge all of that." She stepped to the far side of the room. "I'm going to put you into small groups, and your project will involve not only testing your own comfort zones, but also testing those of others. The project will involve various experiments you will design to disrupt social norms—nothing illegal, unethical, or immoral, folks," she warned. "But do push the envelope and try to think outside the box. Have fun with it."

As she moved up and down the aisles, grouping people, I realized she was assigning people by their spots in the rows. There was a 50 percent chance I was going to be paired up with Benjamin.

Finally, she made it to my row. She grouped the first three people, and then she pointed to Benjamin, me, and Carter.

"Now that you have your groups, here's your assignment. Today I want you to brainstorm ideas on how you can disrupt public norms, plus ideal locations to do your experiment. Your end goal will be to record and analyze how your targets react to your actions in comparison to how you anticipated they would react. Group up!"

Chairs scraped as people formed small clusters around the room.

Benjamin turned his chair around, and I rotated mine to face the middle of the room. Carter kept his facing forward, and his head was propped up in his hands.

I cleared my throat in a lame attempt to get my nerves under control. But I couldn't deny the twinge of eagerness in my heart. I was going to be doing an out-of-school experiment with Benjamin. And Carter, too, but we all knew he'd do the absolute bare minimum, if even that.

"So," I started as I whipped my notebook to a blank page. "Um, anyone have any ideas?" Brilliant, Camilla.

After a moment, Benjamin said, "Let's take a few minutes to jot down some ideas on our own. Then we can discuss them, pick the strongest." The voice of reason.

I gave a dumb nod and bent over my paper.

Carter gave a soft grunt, and out of the corners of my eyes I saw his head nod a few times, getting closer and closer to his desk.

Think, I ordered myself. *Outside the box. Be creative.* I stared at my paper and willed myself to come up with something awesome. What situations would make others uncomfortable?

Oh, say, like a televised promposal?

I smothered an uncomfortable laugh. It was bad enough going through it myself. I wouldn't want to subject anyone else to that kind of misery.

I wrote down a couple of ideas. Stared at the page another long minute. Wrote another one down.

"Got anything?" Benjamin asked.

Thud. Carter's head hit the desk.

I rolled my eyes. "That's about what I expected from him. Anyway, I wrote down, 'Stand too close to someone,' 'Have a public argument,' 'Propose marriage randomly,' and 'Stare at people.'"

He chuckled and my heart flipped at the rich sound. "I wrote, 'Try to hold hands with strangers,' 'Do a survey with uncomfortably personal questions,' and 'PDA.'"

Public displays of affection? My breathing grew shallow at the thought of kissing Benjamin where anyone could see us, his eyes boring into mine as his head tilted and his mouth grew closer, closer . . .

"Well, Carter might not be that into you," I replied to cover my crazy train of thought.

His grin grew. "He'd probably sleep through the whole thing anyway. It would be like kissing Sleeping Beauty. But with itchy facial hair."

I chuckled. Wow, he was funnier than I anticipated. It made

me want to keep talking to see what he'd say or do. This whole class period was keeping me on my toes wondering what was next.

"Class is about to end," Mrs. Brandwright declared. For once, I actually regretted the end of the school day. "Take one more minute. Narrow your list down to your top three disruptive activities. Write them down on a fresh piece of paper, add your names to the paper, and hand it in to me before you go."

Carter gave a soft snore, and Benjamin and I exchanged a raised-eyebrow look.

"I guess it falls on our shoulders," I said, then glanced down at my sheet. "Um, which ones do you like the most? I like your suggestion of trying to hold people's hands." And, of course, I desperately liked the kissing idea, but there was no way in hell I was going to admit that to him.

"I like the idea of standing or sitting too close to people. And the public argument as well."

"Let's go with those, then." I wrote them down and added all three of our names. Then glanced back up at him through my eyelashes. Benjamin wasn't looking at me, his attention back on his notebook.

The last bell rang. The usual end-of-the-day fuss commenced as people grabbed their stuff and ran out of the room. I dropped our paper off on Mrs. Brandwright's desk and then left as well, making sure to nestle myself in the middle of the pack. Not that I anticipated another promposal, but I had a paranoid fear of Zach trying something else wacky to get me to say yes to a date with him.

Speaking of . . . I dug my phone out of my purse. *Five* more messages waiting for me. Seriously? I should have thought more about giving him my number, because all this was doing was making me irritated at him and making me *not* want to be his friend. I'd had no idea he'd blow up my phone like this. I scanned the texts.

Okay, looking forward to it! Hope class is good.

Maybe we can see a movie on Friday?

What shade of red did you mean—like, blood or brick or something closer to pink?

Do you like limos? I'm just curious. Or I could borrow my brother's car.

Sorry, am I bugging you? I'm bugging you, aren't I?

I groaned. I wasn't ready to answer these yet. I headed to my locker and flicked open the lock to get my backpack out. My brain was spinning with everything that had happened in psych. Benjamin had actually talked to me—and not just out of obligation. He'd passed me a note. Had drawn me a picture.

I dug it out and, with the note hidden in my locker, peered at it again. Then I got the perfect idea for what to write in the thought bubble. Joshua would be so proud of me. I quickly scribbled inside it, gathered my stuff, and slammed the door. My pulse throbbed in my throat as I turned the corner and headed toward Benjamin's locker.

Yes, I knew which one was his. I was *that* girl.

The hall was almost empty. I leaned against the row of lockers and pretended to dig through my bag, waiting until people filtered out. When all was clear, I stuck the note through the slot on the top of his locker. The soft plunk let me know it landed.

Then I opened my phone and replied, *Not bugging, but I *am* super busy this week. Sorry. Will msg you later with my answers.*

I donned my gloves and scarf, zipped my coat, and walked out the school door. The sun was surprisingly warm, and I turned my face toward it, basking in the much-needed rays. Spring was finally starting to feel like spring. Things weren't perfect, but they were looking up. Thinking about what I wrote in the comment bubble, I smiled.

I'd given Benjamin my phone number, along with the message *For planning epic social disruption.*

CHAPTER SIX

Joshua

I sighed as I poked the crust of the limp, greasy pepperoni pizza. This was what I got for forgetting to pack my lunch today. "Nasty," I whispered to Camilla. "Pretty sure that isn't real cheese."

She shrugged and grabbed a plate, plopping it onto her tray. "Better than the ham salad sandwich I brought. Mom won't buy more lunch meat until we finish it all."

Camilla's mom *loved* ham salad. She even had her own grinder. Needless to say, Camilla had confessed to me that she'd burned out on it when she was little and now tried to avoid it as often as possible. To the point of packing multiple ham sandwiches she threw away once she got to school, just to fake like she was eating it so she wouldn't hurt her mom's feelings.

At least my dad didn't make me eat crap I didn't want.

I grabbed a spinach salad that didn't look too heinous and put a dollop of ranch dressing on top, then snagged a Coke and a slice of cake. After paying, Camilla and I made our way to our lunch table, where most of the gang was already gathered. David, one of our friends, gnawed on a sandwich, while Niecey and Dwayne sucked on each other's faces, as usual.

No Ethan yet.

The tightness in my shoulders that I hadn't even known was there managed to loosen a touch. Camilla and I sat down and started eating.

She bit into her pizza and frowned. I could see the puddle of grease pooled in one of the curled pieces of pepperoni. "Okay," she mumbled around her bite. "This wasn't my best idea ever."

David laughed. "You're a brave woman," he declared. "I swore off school pizza back in middle school, when I got a slice that was still half frozen." He shuddered in mock horror, his brown eyes twinkling.

I picked at the slivers of mushrooms in my salad. I wasn't really hungry, hadn't eaten much since Saturday night's fiasco with Ethan. I'd managed to avoid him at lunch yesterday, had tried to keep my texts light and relaxed. But my heart was still sick and hurting over the whole situation.

"You okay?" David asked, a frown marring his usually bright face. "You seem a little . . . off."

Even Niecey and Dwayne pulled away from each other to eye me, their mouths swollen and red from so much nonstop kissing.

I waved the fork in the air and forced a wide, fake smile. "Who, me? Why, I'm just perfect."

"Whew," Ethan said as he dropped his brown-paper-bag lunch on the table and took the seat close beside me. "I thought I'd never get out of there. Mrs. Quinton kept me after German class and wouldn't stop talking."

"Hey, Ethan," Camilla said with a small wave.

"Hey there, princess," he replied, then gave David, Niecey, and Dwayne a broad smile. My heart pinged in my chest.

Niecey and Dwayne looked around to make sure there weren't any teachers present, then went back to kissing, arms tangled around each other.

"So, where have you been?" Ethan asked me. He grabbed a bag of baked barbecue chips and ripped it open.

"What?"

"Normally, you text me a lot in your morning classes. Did you get busted and have your phone taken away?"

"Oh. Uh, no." My face burned. I swallowed. I guess my attempts at subtle avoidance weren't working well. "I got busy taking notes and stuff, that's all."

The heat from his nearby thigh seeped into mine, and it was so hard not to just inch my leg over a fraction, see what happened if our knees brushed each other. Would he pull away? Why didn't he feel this crackle between us that I did?

Oh, that's right. Because he felt it for someone else. For perfect, beautiful Noah.

I poked my salad and drew my leg closer to me.

Ethan leaned toward me and whispered in my ear, "Seriously, what's going on with you today? You don't seem like yourself."

The warm puffs of breath caressed my hair and made goose bumps rise across my skin. "What? Me? I'm totally fine." *Liar.* "Just tired. Overschooled. Undersexed. Going through menopause. I'm pregnant. Something dramatic and amazing."

Camilla snorted as she chewed on another bite of her pizza.

Ethan's eyes narrowed. "You're doing that thing."

"Thing?" I blinked.

"Where you turn up the humor. It usually means you're hiding something. What's wrong?"

Shit. I poked my chocolate cake. My heart slammed against my rib cage, and the roar of the students around us melded with the screaming in my head. I was torn between feeling stupidly vulnerable and kind of honored that Ethan knew me so well. "Well," I drawled in a thick mock-Southern accent. What should I say? "I just—"

"Oh my God, she's here," David said, interrupting me. His attention was locked on the cafeteria doors. He tugged a large bag out from under the cafeteria table.

"What are you doing?" Camilla asked him.

"Embracing my destiny." Okay, David was a bit dramatic, but the guy meant well and had a good heart. He stood from the seat, his lanky six-foot-four frame towering over us, cloth bag-straps gripped in his shaking hands. "Wish me luck."

Our whole table—even Niecey and Dwayne—spun around to face the cafeteria doors. There stood Karen, head of the Mathletes, chess captain, girls' rugby cocaptain, tennis captain, and probably leader of many other school groups I didn't even know existed. Her red hair flamed in a rippling cascade of waves, and she was flanked by her two best friends, Ashley and Monica.

"Oh my God," Camilla whispered to me and Ethan. "I think we're about to see another promposal."

Saved from Ethan's inquisition by fate. I avoided looking at him and kept my attention focused on the scene.

The air in the room seemed to shift as David purposefully strolled up to Karen. His long legs ate up the space between them. A foot away from her, he stopped, and she turned from giggling with her friends to peer up into his face.

"Yes?" she asked him with a polite, if not a little frosty, smile.

Whispers fled and darted across the caf. Camilla's hand flew up in front of her mouth as she tensed beside me. Ethan remained strangely still and silent.

"Karen," David said in a loud, rumbling voice. He dropped the bag to his side, dug through it, and whipped out a black top hat. He plopped it on his head and then donned two white gloves.

A couple of girls in the cafeteria giggled, and someone applauded with a loud whistle. Karen's two friends stepped back a touch and began whispering furiously to each other, mouths cupped and eyes locked on the spectacle to come.

Then the room grew eerily quiet. I saw several girls and guys grab their phones and hold them up to video the moment. We all waited to see what David was going to do. Karen's back stiffened, and she frowned. Glanced around and saw the phones stuck in the air.

"I don't—" she started to say.

"Karen," David repeated, "being around you is magic." He flung his gloved hands up in the air with a flourish and then pulled the end of one of those long magic scarves out of his sweater sleeve. So cheesy, but kinda sweet. With a thrust, he crammed the end into Karen's limp hand. "Please pull it."

Dwayne made an under-the-breath comment about something farther south being pulled. Niecey snorted.

"Hmm. No thanks," Karen replied to David. She dropped the end of the scarf.

David's face fell, and my heart stuttered in sympathy for him. Was Karen really going to just let him flounder like this?

With a halting step, Ashley moved forward, bent down, and

took the scarf end. She pulled as brightly toned scarves tied one to another swept out of David's sleeve. Each scarf had a large black letter written on it.

Ashley read the letters out loud until the last scarf came out of the sleeve. "P. R. O. M. P. L. E. A. S. E."

Karen stared on, mixed emotions flying across her face. Her cheeks grew flushed, and she fiddled with her fingers. An uncomfortable feeling settled in my stomach—this was so not going to end well. And the entire thing was going to be captured on video for everyone to see.

But poor David still tried to roll with it. Like a champ, he whipped his hat off and pulled out a bundle of plastic flowers from within, then pushed them toward Karen, who reached out a wooden arm and took them. Her eyes were fixed on the floor.

"Karen, it would be my honor to accompany you to senior prom," he said with loud bravado, though I heard the tremble in his words. "Will you please be my prom date?"

The whole cafeteria went dead silent. I knew what was coming, could see the rejection written all over Karen's eyes and downturned mouth, and I wanted to grab David's arm and yank him out of here. But I couldn't move.

Camilla drew in a soft breath from behind her hand, and Ethan shifted. I dared a glance at him and saw sadness in his eyes. He knew what was coming too.

Karen glanced at Ashley, then at David. She shook her head and handed him back the fake flowers. "No, thanks."

He blinked. "Um, pretty please?"

I cringed. Oh God. This was going downhill, fast. I shifted to stand, thinking of ways I could throw a tarp over David and drag him away, but Camilla grabbed my arm and shot me a warning glance.

Karen sighed and flipped a lock of hair over her shoulder. "Sorry, but I don't want to go to prom with you, David. Not in the least."

Wow. Bitch much? A swell of anger settled like a tight ball in my chest. She didn't need to be so rude about it.

Ashley shot David a worried glance and stepped back. She looked like she wanted to say something but bit her lower lip.

"But . . . I don't . . ." David struggled for words. He twisted the fake flower stems, eyes wide, blinking.

Fervent whispers built to a crescendo around us. "Oh my God. How is he ever going to show his face again around school?" one girl said in a not-so-subtle tone.

"So. Humiliating," another replied.

David licked his lips. He peered around the room and seemed to realize he had a rapt audience witnessing his downfall. "Maybe we can talk about it somewhere else," he offered in a quiet voice.

Karen's eyes flashed. "There's nothing to talk about," she spat out. "I think you've embarrassed me enough for the moment, haven't you? My answer is *no*. I don't want to go to prom with you. I don't like you like that."

Camilla sucked in a shaky breath. "Poor David," she said quietly.

I reached over and patted her leg. She had to be feeling torn right now, given how her own awkward promposal had been sprung on her last week. It was painfully evident Karen was irritated by the surprise, but David was our friend. He had tried so hard to do something sweet to ask her to prom.

David turned away from Karen and with deliberate, careful motions, tucked his hat and gloves back inside his bag. He moved

RHONDA HELMS

around the trio of girls and walked out the cafeteria door. Like his whole world hadn't fallen around his feet right then. In front of so many people who were by now texting everyone else, sending copies of the videos.

We spun back around to face the table and sat in depressed silence for a few moments. Karen and her girls moved toward their table in the corner. No one said a word to Karen or even looked at her. She kept her chin up and didn't talk to anyone.

"Why did you hold me back?" I asked Camilla. "I just wanted to help him."

"This was his moment," she said. "He wouldn't want to be emasculated by having someone rescue him. And I think Karen made herself look bad enough." There was a hint of emotion in her voice, and when I turned to her, I saw her eyes welling up. "And *that* was the exact reason I couldn't say no to Zach. Because I would have looked like a megabitch like her."

"But your no wouldn't have—"

"Holy shit." Niecey shook her head and shot a look at her boyfriend. "That was intense. Poor David. He's gotta be hurting a lot right now."

Ethan, who had been quiet, reached over and touched my forearm. "Hey, you and I still need to talk."

I stood and gathered my stuff. I kept my eyes fixed on my tasks so Ethan couldn't see that the last thing I wanted to do was talk about what was bothering me. "I should go see David. Make sure he isn't jumping off a bridge or something." After I managed to don a broad smile, I looked at him. "I'll catch you later, though, okay?"

His eyes peered into me, and he gave a brief nod.

I knew the best way to get him off my back, and it was going to kill me to pull this card. But it was my only chance of escape. "When we get together, we'll start working on our strategies. For *things*."

The tension around his eyes faded, and he got that dreamy look. "Yeah, that'll be great. Thanks."

It was so hard to gather my pride and keep my chin up. To not smack him on the back of the head and demand he notice me as more than a friend. But this wasn't the time for that. I'd missed my time, and now it was too late.

I told the others bye and took off down the hall for David. If anyone knew the pains of a broken heart, if anyone could commiserate with him right now, it was me.

RHONDA HELMS

CHAPTER SEVEN

Camilla

Hey, Camilla. Did you hear the latest about Karen?" Michelle, the girl kitty-corner to me in psych, leaned forward to whisper to me. She played with the ends of her thick brown braid.

"Beyond what's already buzzing around? Nope." I shook my head and settled into my seat. My stomach was still in knots over that whole debacle three days ago. Luckily, Joshua had hung out with David for a bit after the cafeteria rejection and had managed to get the poor guy to stop hiding out in the bathroom. But videos of the scene were everywhere, all over Facebook and Twitter. Almost couldn't escape it.

While there were a few random douchebags ripping on David for getting shot down, most of the vitriol was aimed at Karen, who seemed to have found herself suddenly infamous over her harsh public rejection. Part of me felt really bad for her, due to the extreme comments being lobbed her way online, but the other part thought she could have handled the whole issue with more care. Like, maybe not be such a bitch, and pull him aside to let him down quietly.

Something I probably should have thought of trying, instead of my nervous agreement to go with Zach. Sigh. Hindsight really was twenty-twenty.

"Well," Michelle said, "my brother said that David's swim teammates swore not to ask her to prom because of how she treated him. And a couple of the other jock circles joined in as well. Some kind of bro solidarity, I guess."

"Wow." Blackballed. Karen had to be upset about that, for sure. What was she going to do?

Benjamin strolled across the front of the room, wearing a pair of perfectly faded jeans and a dark gray T-shirt. My stupid heart did that fluttery thing when our eyes locked. With as much carelessness as I could fake, I turned my attention back to my notebook. After leaving that note in his locker with my number on it, I hadn't heard a peep from him. Not one text.

I was a class-A idiot, obviously. I'd read too much into our in-class interaction on Monday. God, I wished I could go back in time and just not respond at all. Maybe then I wouldn't feel so stupid.

Yet he'd taken the time to draw a sketch of my face. And give it to me. Why do that if he was just going to ignore what I wrote? Maybe I'd slipped the note into the wrong locker, or maybe he never saw it.

Should I ask?

Mrs. Brandwright rushed into the classroom and plopped her stuff down on the desk. "Sorry, guys," she said in a rush. "I had to pop by the library, and then I got distracted talking to teachers. Anyway. I have some lecture material, and then I want you to break into your project groups and start making plans for when you're doing your experiments. The clock is ticking!"

For the next twenty minutes, Mrs. Brandwright went over important notes on social mores and how they evolved over the decades as generations grew up and created new generations with new ideas. It was actually interesting to hear how different things were now from when she was a young kid, such as discussions of money, sex, religion, and politics in mixed-gender company being taboo. Time flew by.

"Okay, that's enough of that." She wiped her chalk-covered hands and laughed when puffs of white floated to the ground. The class laughed too. "Man, do I get messy. Now it's your turn to group together and finalize your plans. As you do, please keep in mind the gender and age of your targets. As I've shown in the lecture, those might impact the reaction you get and are worth noting." After giving us a few more reminders about when the project was due, plus suggestions on where we could go, she waved us into our groups.

We made our small circle again, and I grabbed a fresh piece of paper. Benjamin's knee brushed against my lower thigh, and I swallowed. Grabbed my pencil tighter to keep from leaning toward him.

"Well, Mrs. Brandwright had some good suggestions for where to go to meet a variety of people. Like a park, the mall, or a shopping plaza. Do you guys have a preference?" I looked at Carter, who shrugged. Eh, at least he was awake.

Benjamin rubbed his jaw without looking at me. "Mall would be fine." He flipped his notebook open and began writing a few notes.

Okay. Succinct as ever. I shoved down the flare of disappointment in his deliberate lack of attention toward me. Obviously, he wanted to make sure I didn't get any further mixed signals. *Message received, dude.* I made a mental note to stop acting so interested in whatever he was doing.

"Mall it is, then." I summed up what our chosen activities would be on the paper. "And what are our expected outcomes?" We were supposed to predict what we thought people would do, record the actual reactions, then compare and discuss it all.

"I think old people will freak out," Carter offered with a mumble.

I gave an enthusiastic nod at him, glad he was actually participating for once. I wrote his answer down. "Yeah, probably so."

"Probably get mixed reactions from younger people, but they might laugh more than anything," Benjamin offered, his attention still focused on his notebook. The page now had the start of some ornate line work in the margins. As he lifted it to flip to a new page, I saw a book tucked underneath.

I couldn't help it; I tilted my head and peered at the title. *The Canterbury Tales*, written in a fancy swirling medieval script, and I saw the top of a woman's headdress near the upper-right corner. Interesting choice of reading material.

"Are you two free on Sunday?" Benjamin asked, and I blinked and looked away from his desk, guilty at having been caught staring, despite my promise to myself not five minutes ago. So much for acting disinterested in him. I was lame.

I nodded in response to his question.

Carter did as well. He sighed and leaned his head against his hand. Apparently, nodding was hard work for him.

"Let's meet at noon. In the food court." Benjamin dropped his pen and leaned back in his chair, rubbed the back of his neck.

"Sounds good." Curiosity burned in my belly as I peeked once again at the book on his desk. "What are you reading?" I asked, even though I obviously knew the answer. I nodded toward the book hidden under his notebook. The real question I wanted to ask was *why*, but that seemed too open-ended and risky.

"It's for English, but I read it last year during Christmas break. *The Canterbury Tales.*" Benjamin was in advanced English, whereas I was in honors. Different curriculum material. "Have you read it? It's written in Middle English, but it comes with a translation." He took it out and showed me the cover, with a bunch of medieval people riding horses across a hilly landscape.

Apparently, all I needed to do to get him to talk was discuss books. Interesting. "No, our English teacher is firmly contemporary." Ms. Wickliffe preferred for our class to read more modern material, from the twentieth century on. No translations needed in hopes that we'd enjoy the reading more. Plus, as a hard-core feminist, she was super vocal about avoiding the works of dead white guys as much as possible.

His shrug was casual, but I saw a flare of something deeper in his eyes. "It's actually funny. Lots of bawdy old jokes. 'The Wife of Bath's Tale' is one of my favorites."

"That sounds cool. Did you—" I stopped myself right in the nick of time from blurting out to ask if he'd gotten the note with my number. What was with me?

He blinked. "Did I what?"

I shook my head. "Nothing. Never mind." If he did get it, I

didn't want to know why he didn't reply. And if he didn't get it for some reason, maybe it was better that way.

He stared at me for a moment, and I fought the urge to squirm. I just kept my chin up and stared back, like nothing was bothering me. This guy had to suspect he was getting to me, and for some stubborn reason, I didn't want him to know.

After a moment, I saw the edges of a smile creep across his face. "Okay. Be mysterious, then." He gave a quick nod.

I heard a slight snore, and we both turned our heads to see Carter drooping, head hitting the desk. Benjamin's eyes connected with mine again, this time in obvious mutual amusement. My breath caught in my throat at the way his eyes danced. I found myself wanting to know more about this guy. Who he was and why he liked reading such an odd collection of books.

The bell rang. My pulse raced with a strong stutter when I realized I was going to see him on Sunday. Though it was a school project, it would be in a casual environment. A chance to get to know him a little better.

Neither he nor I moved from our desks, though Carter awoke with a snort and gathered his stuff.

"Have a great weekend!" Mrs. Brandwright said as she gathered her belongings too and then followed students out the door.

Benjamin eyed me for a moment longer, and I could tell that he wanted to say something. Instead, he grabbed his belongings and stood. With a quick nod at me, he headed out of the room.

God, that guy was driving me nuts! Looking at me, not looking at me. Talking to me, then not talking to me. Was it any wonder I was so utterly confused? Maybe I should talk to Joshua, see what he thought. He had a wiener; surely he could help translate Man Language for me.

My phone vibrated. I groaned and dug it out of my pocket. Zach had backed off texting as much after I promised we'd talk on the phone this weekend about prom plans, but I'd managed to avoid the date issue so far.

But it wasn't Zach. It was a number I didn't recognize.

I'll be at the mall at 11:30 Sunday. If you want, we can grab lunch and strategize beforehand.

The air locked in my chest. It was Benjamin. Had to be—I hadn't given Carter my number. So he *had* gotten my note.

And he wanted to meet with me before our group meeting.

What did that mean? Was it really just about the project, or was there something else?

Only one way to find out. My stupid fingers trembled like crazy as I typed out, *Okay, see you then.*

I gathered my stuff and walked out of the classroom. Because I'd dawdled so long, the halls were empty except for a few other stragglers. Normally, I'd find Joshua and we'd walk home together, but I knew he was staying late today, so I meandered to my locker. Gathered my things. Walked down the hallway, my feet thudding across the slick gray tiles.

About twenty feet away, I realized I'd headed right to the library. I couldn't blame my subconscious for it; I knew I wanted to check out *The Canterbury Tales* and see what it was all about.

I looked up its code on our library computer and went to the right spot. Found several editions of the book and looked for one with a fairly easy-to-read translation. I gripped the paperback and made my way to the checkout desk right before the library closed for the weekend. I could read a chapter or two before Sunday, like the one on the Wife of Bath, and it might give us something to talk about if conversation turned awkward. God knew Carter wasn't going to be any help in that department, if he even showed up.

I tucked the book into my bag and walked home. Now all I had to do was figure out what the hell I was going to wear that would be casual yet alluring.

CHAPTER EIGHT

Joshua

Dammit." Wrong chord. That sounded like total crap. I strummed the right chord a few times to help my fingers remember, then wrote it down on the blank sheet music. "Much better."

Milkshake meowed her approval and curled up in a tighter fur ball on my pillow.

"Josh," Dad hollered from downstairs, "did you finish the laundry?"

"Yes," I yelled back, glad he couldn't see me rolling my eyes. "Your basket is on your bedroom floor." Where I always put it.

"Oh. Uh, thanks."

Poor man. He always got forgetful when in writing mode. For the next twenty minutes, I focused on writing down and practicing the chords for the new song I was composing. When I heard the oven buzzer go off, I plopped my guitar on my bed and dashed downstairs. The scent of fresh lasagna made my stomach growl.

I whipped off the foil and set the timer for another fifteen minutes. I was ready to destroy this dinner.

I heard my text ringtone go off and realized I'd left my cell on the coffee table before starting guitar practice. I darted into the living room to grab it, opening it to find a message from Ethan.

We need to talk.

My stomach clenched. Dammit, I thought he'd dropped the inquisition, especially since I faked enthusiasm over our tentative ideas like no one's business.

Another message popped up. *I'm outside your door.* Followed by the front doorbell ringing just a few feet from me.

"Josh, can you get that?" Dad asked.

Shit. No running from it now. I tried to affect a casual air when I opened the door. "Hey," I said to Ethan. "Come on in. Um, we're about to eat dinner soon, but you can stay if you want."

He tucked his hands in his jeans pockets, slouching a little as he looked at me from the stoop. "Do you *want* me to stay?"

There was a hint of vulnerability in his eyes that gave me a guilty pinch in my chest. My avoidance was hurting his feelings. "Of course I do." I opened the door wider and ushered him inside. "Besides, I made my world-famous lasagna, and you know there's a ton of it."

The tension in his face relaxed, and he gave me a genuine smile as he took off his coat. "Sounds great."

"Do I hear Ethan?" Dad asked from his office.

"You could see him too if you stopped yelling and got up every once in a while," I teased. Dad was really bad to holler at everyone so he could keep his butt glued in the chair and eke out a few more words.

I heard a loud sigh; then Dad came out of the office, his black hair spiked all over on the top. He gave us both a wide grin. "The boy's getting better at nagging me," he said to Ethan with a laugh and a wink.

Ethan pushed up the green sleeves of his shirt, revealing golden arm hair and lean muscles. I bit back a sigh and turned toward the kitchen. Grabbed three plates and forks, plus cups. Folded napkins, set the table, anything to distract me from Ethan's presence just a few feet away.

"Can I help with anything?" he asked right behind me.

I stiffened and drew in a ragged breath. The scent of his cologne wafted in the air, and it filled me with the urge to bury my nose in his neck. "No. I'm . . . good," I managed to say.

Finally, the timer went off again, and I fussed over the lasagna, cutting perfect-sized pieces and serving them up with dinner rolls. Dad and Ethan sat down at the table, and we dug in.

After taking a particularly large bite, Dad scratched at the thick whiskers on his jaw—he probably hadn't shaved for a few days now.

"You look like a wild man, Mr. Mendez," Ethan said with a chuckle. His own jawline was smooth in contrast. "I haven't seen you so rugged in a while."

"Yeah. Happens every time I get this close to a deadline," he grumbled. "I still have a hundred pages to go, and the book is due to my editor in two weeks."

Ethan gave a serious nod, then shot me a crooked half smile. He was all too familiar with my dad's writing craziness, since I griped about it at times like these. When Mom had divorced him and moved to another city for her job, it was hard to get him out of bed, dressed, showered. Even to get him to eat. But over time, his friends and I encouraged him to get back into his favorite hobby, writing, so he'd have a reason to get up every day.

It worked. Dad finished a book. Got an agent. Got a multibook deal. The hobby Mom had disliked so intensely while they'd been married became his sole method of earning money.

Now I couldn't keep Dad out of the office, but at least he seemed happier. All that angst and frustration and anger he'd felt about Mom had been funneled into his writing craft. He spent hours agonizing over the perfect phrases, the darkest plot twists, and the most sinister characters.

"This lasagna is great," Ethan said to me as he took another bite.

I tried not to watch the way his Adam's apple bobbed when he swallowed, the lean lines of his neck. The curve of his lips wrapped around the fork. But even the mundane seemed entrancing when he did it.

I was ridiculously, hopelessly in love with my best guy friend.

Despite my efforts to take my time eating—knowing that after dinner Ethan and I would be talking—dinner went all too fast. Dad cleared his plate and made a beeline for his office. Which left me and Ethan. Alone.

I rinsed the plates and loaded the dishwasher with Ethan's help. We wrapped up the leftovers. I grabbed two mugs and poured coffee I'd brewed a couple of hours ago, reheated them in the microwave, and then handed him one.

Without speaking, we both moved upstairs into my room, him right behind me. I could feel his eyes on my back, and it made my spine itch. I led him in. He sat on the edge of my bed, while I sat on my computer chair.

His gaze roamed over the sheet music on my bed, the guitar. While he didn't play any music, he loved hearing my songs and often asked me to make one up for him. If only he knew how many I'd written in my head. Ones I could never sing because they spilled all of me, my rawest feelings, my deepest secrets, out for all to hear.

For *him* to hear.

"Can you play it for me?" he asked in a quiet tone.

My heart raced as I reached over and picked up the guitar, then adjusted the sheets for easy viewing. Thankfully, I hadn't gotten to writing down the lyrics yet, so the words could stay safely locked away in my head.

I strummed a few warm-up chords, then began to play. The song was incomplete, but the first two verses and the chorus were there, supported by a dancing bass line. I kept my eyes firmly on the paper and tried not to peek over at Ethan to gauge his reaction.

Would he be able to guess this song was for him? About him? No, he wouldn't assume it.

My fingers fumbled just once, but I quickly recovered and finished what I'd written. When the last chord finished, the music vibrated into the silence, then faded away. We sat there without speaking for a couple of minutes, and I dared a glance at Ethan's face. There was an intensity in his eyes; he'd been staring at me the whole time.

My throat tightened. I rested the guitar on my lap. "I still have to write more."

"And lyrics, right? It was gorgeous. What's it about?"

Oh, not much. Just about you and how crazy I am about you. A hot flush crept up my cheeks. "I don't know yet." God, I hated lying to him.

Ethan shifted on the bed and gave a heavy sigh. His eyes turned sad. "You don't like him, do you."

I didn't need to ask who he was talking about. I knew who he meant. Noah, the guy who was on his mind, who occupied his heart. "That's not it." That part was true. Noah wasn't a bad person; in fact, he was generally nice to everyone. No one had a legit complaint about how he treated them.

Didn't change the fact that I wanted Ethan for myself.

"Then why are you being so weird? Ever since I told you last weekend that I wanted to ask him to prom, you've been strange." He rested his hands in his lap.

I put the guitar away in its case and put the sheet music back in my folder. My brain scrambled for the right words, the ones that would soothe him but not give away how I really felt. After all, the truth wasn't an option here.

"It's because I asked you to help me with the promposal, isn't it?" I heard a tinge of emotion in his voice and looked over at him. He was staring at the wall behind me. "It put you in a weird spot, like I was dumping my issues on your shoulders. I'm sorry I didn't realize it before."

True, yet not true. My mouth filled with unspoken words I struggled to bite back.

Ethan turned angst-filled eyes to me and stood. "I'm sorry, man. Of course you don't have time to help me with this. I never meant it to get in the way of our friendship." He turned toward the door.

"No, don't," I blurted out.

Dammit. I couldn't let him think he was a jerk for asking a friend to help. Why would he think otherwise? Friends helped each other. God knew he'd helped me more times than I could count.

I shoved aside my selfish emotions. I had to help Ethan, had to put my feelings on the back burner. My friend needed me, to the point where he even felt guilty about asking me to assist him. Afraid it would come between us.

Ethan was no user. And I was an ass to make him feel that way.

God, this was going to suck. But it was the right thing to do.

He frowned as he looked at me. Crossed his arms.

I bit my lip and gave a casual shrug. "I'm an idiot. I feel way out of my league with planning promposals and I'm afraid of letting you down." To a degree, that was true. Though just a small sliver of the whole truth.

His shoulders relaxed, and the tension lines around his mouth eased. One eyebrow rose. "You? A failure at planning something amazing?" A smile crept onto his face as he shook his head in disbelief.

I pressed a hand to my chest and sniffed. The bubble of sorrow grew bigger, but I shoved it down, focused instead on the relief that my friend was no longer filled with anxiety about us. "I know. But I do have *some* mortal flaws, you know, though they're few and far between."

Ethan moved back to the bed and sat down. "I have no idea how to go about this. He's barely noticed my existence. How do I craft a promposal that won't freak him out or make him reject me?"

"He'd be an idiot to turn you down," I said in full honesty. "But first things first. The best way for us to make your promposal amazing is to make it personal. We need to find out what we can about him. Let's start with you telling me what you already know."

About five minutes into this exercise, I regretted it and wanted to chew off my own hand. I learned that Noah always eats healthy meals at school, that he has all As and Bs in his classes, he's left-handed and likes to tutor students who need help in English. Even his damned fingers were perfect. No chewed nails, unlike mine, which were a hot mess because of my anxiety over Ethan this week. I curled my hands around my pen even more to hide them from view.

"Well, that gives us a place to start," I said. I dropped the pen and leaned back in my chair.

"Thank you," Ethan said. His voice wasn't light and peppy but deep, full of emotion. He leaned forward, resting those lean forearms on his sturdy thighs, and peered up at me. "I couldn't do this without you."

"Yes, you could." I gave him my best crooked grin. "But I'm here for you."

We spent another half hour or so bullshitting about every-thing and nothing. Once the topic of Noah was dropped, our friendship slid back into its easy existence, the way it always had. Yapping about our baseball team and who had the best stats so far, how progress with the senior musical was going, which classes were giving us headaches. Who had the tightest ass on the soccer team.

Ethan glanced at his watch. He rolled his eyes. "Shit. Gotta watch my sister tonight. Parents are going to a concert and asked me to babysit."

Which meant Darlene, his eight-year-old sister, would spend all evening hounding Ethan to play Barbies and dress-up.

I snorted. "Have fun, Prince Ken."

He shoved my arm. "Shut up, or I'll make you join us."

Part of me was tempted, as goofy as it sounded.

I escorted him to the door and watched Ethan walk down the sidewalk toward his car, coat draped over his arm. He got in and drove off.

I stood there in the doorway for a couple of minutes, trying to smile, trying to pretend I wasn't making what felt like the biggest sacrifice of my life.

CHAPTER NINE

Camilla

I popped my last cold French fry in my mouth and kept an eye on the main food court doors. No sign of Carter. We'd been waiting a half hour for him to show, sitting at the table in semi-awkward silence, just watching people walk by.

Benjamin sipped his soda. "He's not coming."

"Big shocker there." I tossed my trash, then sat back down. It was hard not to feel deflated, and we hadn't even started our project yet. When Benjamin had asked me to show up early, I'd thought it meant we were going to spend some time talking beforehand. Maybe getting to know each other or something. Instead, he'd been all business, ironing out which parts of the mall were the best populated for our purposes, which experiment we should try first, and so on.

"We should go ahead and get started." He stood, dumped his empty cup. "Time's a-wastin'."

I shoved aside my feelings and put on my game face. Today was going to be all about school. At least I knew it up front so there wasn't any confusion. I squared my shoulders. "Sounds good."

We headed to one wing, where younger teens and adults were milling around from store to store. He and I had decided we were going to try the random hand-holding in this area. My palms got sweaty from nerves, but I wiped them on my jeans and took in a steadying breath. My blood thrummed in my veins.

I hadn't anticipated how afraid I'd be to do this. Not only were we challenging others, but we were challenging ourselves.

A hand landed on my shoulder, and I turned around. Benjamin stared down at me, green eyes tinged with a hint of concern. "It'll be fine," he said. "Odds are, most people will laugh or back away. Just remember it's for a project—it's not personal."

It was hard not to take this all personally when I was feeling so keyed up . . . and when his thumb was pressing into the dent above my collarbone. I swallowed, nodded. Tried not to savor the warmth of his skin flowing through my shirt to my own flesh.

He gave me a small smile, and the knot of tension in my belly unwound just a bit. His hand squeezed for just a moment; then he stepped back. "Okay, ready?"

I nodded again, this time with more confidence. "I'll go first." We'd decided during our planning session that we'd take turns doing each assignment, and the observing person would take notes.

I walked up to a teen walking with his girlfriend. There was a gap between them, so I slipped into it and gripped both of their hands. "Hey," I said with a big smile.

Their steps stalled for a moment, and their eyebrows were clear up to their hairlines. Then they both gave uncomfortable laughs. "Um, do I know you?" the girl asked me.

I shook my head and let go of their hands. "Have a great day!" Then I spun around and hustled toward Benjamin, who had a huge grin on his face. "Oh my God, that was so weird," I whispered to him. I was buzzing with adrenaline now. When I peeked over my shoulder at the couple, I saw them laughing hard as they walked hand in hand, and a warm feeling surged over me.

I'd done it.

The next hour flew by, and we finished our hand-holding experiment, followed by sitting or standing too close to others. I could see Benjamin had a different approach from mine as he tackled each project, and I tried to glean whatever info about him I could from my observations. Whereas I nervously giggled or found myself acting goofy, he was cool as a cucumber. Just slid up to people and began conversations as if they were lifelong friends.

Most of our targets blinked in surprise but started talking right back to us, though a few people shot us wary glances and stepped away as quickly as they could. One woman yelled at Benjamin, a scowl on her old face, but when he held up his hands with a friendly smile and spoke in a soothing tone under his breath, she lost her hostile edge and eventually smiled back.

The guy continued to surprise me.

We decided to take a break before beginning the public argument part of our experiment. I was craving Orange Julius like crazy, so we walked over to the kiosk and I ordered two.

When I got mine, I took a big draw and sighed with pleasure. "Perfection in a cup."

"I've never had one," he said, eyeing his cup.

"That's downright un-American," I declared. "I insist you do so immediately." Watching him hold hands with strangers and sit really close to them had broken some kind of wall between us. Or maybe my nervous filter was down, because I found myself talking like he and I were lifelong friends too. Not worrying for the moment about how he was viewing me.

His eyebrow rose but he took a sip. Then another. "Okay, that is pretty good."

I gave a satisfied nod. "Told ya."

We strolled over to a bench in the middle of the mall and sat down to finish our drinks. I was so nervous, I chugged mine, then tossed the cup in a nearby garbage can. I could feel the heat pouring off his side, he was so close to me. Guess the whole personal boundaries experiment wasn't quite over after all. Or maybe he wasn't aware he was that close to me. Or—

"You're thinking hard," he said.

"What?"

"I can tell when something's on your mind."

I bit my lower lip. Crap, was I that obvious? "How?"

"You get this faraway look in your eye, like you're having these deep thoughts. And you play with your fingers." He nodded at my hands.

I glanced down at my lap. Sure enough, my fingers were twisted together. I separated them, then sat on my hands, palms down. "I read 'The Wife of Bath's Tale,'" I said in a desperate attempt to divert the conversation.

He leaned back just a touch and eyed me. I could see surprise glinting in his eyes. "Really? What did you think?"

"It made me laugh. They were pretty naughty. I wouldn't have guessed it." I chuckled. "I'm going to read some of the other tales tonight."

I could see his throat working, his Adam's apple bobbing, as he kept staring at me. "You're an interesting person, Camilla."

My chest tightened. "How so?" I managed to squeak out.

"I just . . . never know what to expect, I guess."

Same here. It was so hard not to sway closer to him, to those tempting lips, and just press one tiny little minuscule kiss there. Just to see what would happen. I pressed my hands into my lap again, purposely planting my palms on my thighs to keep them in place.

My text ringtone went off. I ignored it—whoever it was could wait. "Do you have any brothers or sisters?" I asked him when the sound died down.

He shot a curious glance at my jeans pocket, where my phone was nestled, but didn't say anything. "An older brother. He's in college. You?"

I shook my head. "Just me and my parents. Where do you want to go to school after you graduate?"

A fraction of a pause; then he said, "I'm probably going to stay local."

"I'm not sure where I'm going," I confessed. "I have some options, but I don't know what the right choice is." Part of me wanted to stay home and be near my family, but I felt like I should take advantage of college and go away somewhere.

"What do you want to do?"

"I want to teach history."

He blinked. "Interesting. Why?"

"It fascinates me. I've always been intrigued by what came before us. What events and people led us to this very moment, and how different people spin various interpretations of our past. I really like American history in particular." Crap, I was rambling. *Shut up, Camilla.*

He shifted a bit toward me, and I could feel his warm breath caressing my heated cheeks. "You're not what you seem," he finally said. I could hear a hint of admiration in his voice. "I don't know what I want to do in school. I can't narrow it down to something," he admitted. "That's part of the reason why I'm having a hard time deciding where to go."

My throat closed up as we stared at each other. I saw flecks of brown in his eyes, locked dead onto mine. My pulse pounded in my ears. It was almost hard to believe we were really here, talking like this. His eyes darted oh-so-briefly to my lips, and I drew in a shaky breath.

Kiss me, I willed him. *Please.*

Something flickered in his eyes, and he stood. Cleared his throat. "We should finish this last part."

"Oh. Right. Yeah." I gathered my notebook and straightened. Steadied myself, smoothed my sweater. "Time to get into a fight."

"Holy crap," I said with a gush of laughter. I leaned my back against the narrow hallway's smooth brick interior. "That was unreal."

Even Benjamin was chuckling. He stood opposite me, one foot kicked up on the brick, arms crossed. "I'm just glad we didn't get the mall cops called on us."

For the last half hour, we'd moved around the mall and staged fake fights, letting impulse and inspiration dictate the argument topic. So I picked a fight with him on how we never went to the burger places I loved. He argued with me that I was too clingy and never let him hang with his parents.

Over-the-top, ridiculous arguments. It was hard not to snort with laughter the whole time. But the people around us did as we predicted, for the most part—avoided eye contact and walked away.

Now we had ducked into a hallway between the hair salon and the department store to pause and write notes. I slid down to sit on the floor and whipped out my pen. Scratched my hasty notes on a sheet of paper so I wouldn't forget.

"Nice job," I told him when I finished. I capped my pen and put the notebook away in my large purse. "You had me convinced you hated tofu."

He smirked. "And you truly made me believe you couldn't stand my mom. Though she'd be crushed if she ever learned that."

My heart was still racing from the experiment. I stood right in front of him and peered up. "You can tell her I'll take her out to dinner in apology. If she'll even let me back in after I threw her homemade sweater in her face. That really was rude of me."

Something dark flashed in his eyes, and then his head dropped down and his mouth touched mine.

I froze for a second and gave a small, shocked gasp. One of his hands reached across my lower back to tug me closer, and the other pressed against the back of my head.

Benjamin was kissing me.

I deepened the kiss, tasted him, breathed in his rich scent. Tangled my fingers in the thick hair at the nape of his neck. Blood coursed through my veins, lit up my senses, and set me on fire. I could almost hear my own heart pounding.

"Ooooh!" a light, feminine voice called out from the hallway entrance.

Benjamin and I jumped apart, panting, staring at each other in surprise.

The young woman, dressed all in black, strolled toward the

side door that led into the salon. "By all means, don't let me stop you," she teased, then headed in.

When we were alone again, Benjamin scrubbed a hand across his face. "Shit," he said. "I . . . Camilla . . ." His gaze danced everywhere but on me.

God, he must not have meant to do that. "Guess we can add PDA to our list after all," I said with more bravado than I felt. I forced a laugh. "Mrs. Brandwright will be proud. We might even get extra credit."

Some of the stress seeped from his spine, and he finally looked at me. His smile was small, but I could tell he was trying to ease the awkwardness that sat between us like a massive elephant.

I could still feel the heat of his mouth on mine, his hands searing my skin. Apparently, I was the only one who'd enjoyed that encounter. So why had he done it, then? Why had he kissed me? Was it because he'd gotten passionately riled up from our fake fights? And now he regretted it?

I shoved off and headed down the hall. Looked back at him over my shoulder with a casual air, though my heart was chipping into small, embarrassed pieces. "I don't know about you, but I need a pretzel."

His face was impossible to read as he moved toward me, stepped in place by my side. We walked through the mall at a leisurely pace. He stayed quiet. I pretended he hadn't rocked my world with that amazing, intoxicating kiss. Then crushed it with his obvious regret.

The pretzel station had a line. I waited, fidgeted. Suddenly, I was anxious to get out of there. I needed to regroup, to gather my wits and stop thinking about this guy.

I could still taste him on my lips.

I got the damn pretzel and ate it as fast as I could. We continued our walk toward the food court, passing a tux store.

The question burned in my head. I wasn't going to ask. Nope. It didn't matter if he was or not.

But my stupid mouth opened, and before I realized it, I asked, "So, are you going to prom?"

He gave a casual shrug. "Probably not. I've never been much into dances." He paused. "So how long have you and Zach been dating?"

I stopped in place and barked out a laugh. Was *that* why he was now acting so weird? "What? No, we're not dating."

"But you're going to prom with him." His face was a mask as he turned to me.

It was on the tip of my tongue to say, "Because he forced me into it by asking me in front of everyone!" but that wasn't entirely true. After all, I did say yes to him. I couldn't put it all on his shoulders. "We're . . . friends." Kinda.

"Are you sure he understands that?"

Why wouldn't he? I hadn't given him any mixed signals. Unlike this guy, who blew hot and cold every five minutes. I walked up to Benjamin and eyed him hard. "I—"

My phone rang out with my text tone. Crap. I dug it out and saw I had a couple of texts from Zach—he must have been the one who'd texted me earlier. Speak of the devil. My lips thinned as I eyed the screen.

Busy? Whatcha doin?

Hey, we're having chicken for dinner. If you're not busy, come over.

I huffed a sigh, stuck my phone back in my pocket. When I glanced up, Benjamin was giving me a knowing look.

"Three guesses who's been blowing up your phone today," he said with a low chuckle as he shook his head. But his eyes were a little flat. Or maybe I was just imagining it because I wanted to think he didn't like even the idea of me dating Zach. "You might not think you're dating, Camilla, but it looks like he does."

I swallowed a groan. I was going to have to nip this in the bud with Zach before it got worse. The hard part was going to be figuring out how without making myself look like a total bitch.

Fun times, indeed.

CHAPTER TEN

Joshua

I love your hair," I told Camilla at lunch. It was sleeked back in a ponytail, not her usual style, but it worked well with the lean lines of her black-clad figure today.

"Thanks."

Hmm. Normally, she was much more enthusiastic when I complimented her. "Your nails look good too."

She gave a short nod. "Did them yesterday morning."

"And that sandwich looks divine."

She gave a halfhearted shrug as she eyed the turkey sandwich on top of her brown paper bag. "It's okay."

"All right, what is wrong with you?" All day she'd been off. Slumping around, not talking much, barely even smiling.

"I just . . ." She heaved a sigh and finally turned to look at me. Her eyes showed signs of fatigue, and there were frown lines around her mouth. She dropped her voice and said, "I'll talk to you about it later, okay? It's not something I want to discuss here in front of everyone."

I rubbed her back. It hurt to see her so down when she was

always such an upbeat person. Something was really eating at her. "Okay. But I'm holding you to that."

The two of us went back to eating in silence. Dwayne fed Niecey small pieces of cheese in between covering her face with kisses. Given the way Camilla kept her attention resolutely focused on anything but them, I could tell that her problem had to do with love woes. Most likely something about Benjamin or Zach.

Ethan wasn't here today—probably doing some kind of tutoring—so I cleared my throat and looked at David. "How ya doing? Feeling any better?" Luckily, the furor regarding his promposal disaster had died down for the most part. Since a junior couple had been caught having sex in the janitor's closet on Thursday, the drama had shifted elsewhere.

He shrugged and ate a chip. "Can't complain. Grandma's finally out of the hospital and doesn't have to have surgery. And my brother's coming home from Iraq next month too."

His positivity in the face of such public embarrassment made my heart pinch with shame. Here I was, dwelling on my own misery about Ethan, but he wasn't sitting here all butt-hurt about being dissed. No, he was grateful for his family.

Even Camilla straightened her spine and offered him a thin smile. "I'm so happy to hear that," she said, her voice ringing with sincerity. "Your brother was a senior when we were freshmen, wasn't he? I seem to remember him. Always a nice guy."

David nodded, and his face warmed up more. "Yeah, he loved this school. Though, I have to admit, I'm kinda glad he wasn't here to witness me getting shredded for my promposal. Guess I need to work on my magic tricks a bit more." He gave a dry laugh.

We all chuckled.

"If you can't laugh at yourself . . ." He trailed off and looked over my shoulder. "What is she doing?"

Camilla and I spun around and peered at the cafeteria doorway. There stood Ashley, wearing a kid's princess crown on top of fake blond curls. In one hand was a huge pink wand with a light-up star at the top.

People in the cafeteria started giggling.

Ashley's face was beet red, but she lifted her chin and walked toward our table. Her friends, sitting at their own table—including Karen, who was shooting death rays via her eyes—sat there in silence.

"Hey, David," she said and waved the wand in the air.

"Uh, hi." His smile grew wider.

Ashley lifted her other arm, and I noticed the large white poster board. She held it over her head. On the front was written in puffy purple letters, PROM? "So. Um. David, I don't know if you got a date to prom, but if not . . ." She swallowed and drew in a shaky breath. "I'd like to go with you. Uh, if you'd go with me, I mean. If we could go together—"

"That would be great." He stood, and the smile on his face was so wide I could practically see his back teeth. "Yes. I'd love to go to prom with you."

Everyone in the cafeteria started clapping. Ashley dropped the poster board back down to her side and stood there awkwardly as David made his way to her. The two of them whispered a bit. Camilla and I turned back to face the table and give them a little privacy.

"Okay, that was sweet," she said, giving her first real Camilla smile of the day. "I'm glad to see someone appreciating David. He's a doll."

I shot a glance at Karen, who was still staring at Ashley and David. "She's pissed. But I can't figure out why."

Camilla frowned and glared at Karen until the girl looked away and started whispering to the blonde on her right. "Probably because she's a megabitch and she can't stand for anyone to be happy."

Ashley and David sat down at our table, and she tossed the wand onto the Formica surface. Her cheeks were still red, but flushed with pleasure. She didn't look back at Karen or her usual table, just stayed in place while David got up and stood in the lunch line.

When Karen saw him leave, she rose from her table and stomped over. "What the hell are you doing?" she barked at Ashley in a loud whisper as she slid into the seat on the girl's left.

"Oh, hello, Karen," I said to her in a droll tone. "We're all doing well; thanks for asking."

She rolled her eyes at me, then turned her attention back to her friend. "Yeah. Anyway, why would you ask *him* to prom?" Her eyes flashed to the lunch line. "Brian's been telling everyone he's going to ask you any day now. And you totally just killed that opportunity."

Ashley sighed and pressed her fingers to her brow. "I don't like Brian—he's not my type. Besides, you're the one always trying to force him on me. He's barely said more than a sentence or two to me all year."

"Seriously, though. David? Of everyone in this school, *he's* your 'type'?" She glanced around and seemed to realize she was sitting among David's friends, all of whom were glaring at her. Even Niecey and Dwayne had pried themselves apart enough to snarl in her direction. Karen stopped talking and pursed her lips.

"I think you should go," Ashley said, quiet but resolute. "This isn't up for discussion. I'm going with David to prom."

"You've just committed social suicide." Karen stood and tossed her head back. Looked down her nose at all of us. "Have fun." She strolled back to her table.

"Well, that was straight out of an eighties movie," Camilla said.

Ashley gave a nervous titter. She peeked at the cafeteria line, then back at us. "I'm sorry about that. She can be a real jerk sometimes." She gnawed on her thumbnail.

"It's not your fault," I said quietly. "And it's fine. I promise. She's just feeling embarrassed because you showed her up by being such a good person. You made her look even douchier than she already did."

"Shit." She frowned. "I didn't mean to do that. I just . . ."

"You just what?" David slid into the seat beside her, holding a tray bearing two slices of cake. He handed her one. "What did I miss?"

She waved her hand and offered David a broad smile. "Oh. It was nothing. This cake looks delicious. Thanks."

Ashley and David spent the rest of the lunch period in shy conversation. It was so cute I almost couldn't stand it. The furtive glances, the awkward smiles, the flushed faces. How had I missed before that Ashley had a crush on David? I was usually pretty good at spotting these things.

Then again, I'd been *totally* blindsided by Ethan's crush on Noah, so there was that.

The bell rang. We dumped our trash. I gave Camilla a hug and whispered in her ear to text me when she got a chance, then headed out of the caf into the hallway. A hand on my upper arm stopped me in place.

"Hey." Ethan huffed a few breaths and leaned over, looking winded. "Shit. I missed lunch. Needed to talk."

I laughed. "Take a moment and catch your breath, dude."

He chuckled and stood, drew in a few deep lungfuls of air. "Okay. Sorry. I ran all the way here from the other side of the school."

To find *me*? I wanted to be flattered, but I had a hunch it wasn't really about me. It was about the guy not twenty feet in front of us, going up to his locker to flick the lock. Beautiful, stunning, funny, smart, fill-in-your-own-gushy-adjective Noah.

I gave him a polite smile and tamped down my disappointment. "What's up?"

"When can we start brainstorming for real? I need to get on it. Are you free this week?"

Bingo. I called it. I should go into gambling. Or open a psychic hotline. I grabbed my phone and peeked at the calendar. "I'm free Wednesday after school."

"Perfect." Ethan gave a crooked smile, and the sight of that damned dimple made my heart skip a beat. Why did he have to be so . . . everything to me? How was I going to learn how to stop loving this guy? About as easy as asking me to rip my heart out of my chest and still keep on living.

Ethan finally spotted Noah, and I saw minuscule changes in his body language—the way his eyes widened, how he sucked in his breath and clenched his fists at his sides. Did his nervous stomach flutter mirror my own?

"I want to talk to him," Ethan whispered to me, "but I don't know what to say. I'd like to break the ice before I just outright ask him to prom." He turned desperate, wide eyes my way. "Help, please."

My heart gave a sick thud. I kept my smile glued in place so as not to give away my feelings. "You guys have a class together, right? Why not ask him if you can borrow his notes? Something casual that gives you a chance to see him again and discuss what he wrote."

"That's brilliant." He reached up and squeezed my arm. His eyes were rich and warm with affection. "Thank you. Wish me luck!" With that, he strolled over to Noah, who looked at him with a smile when Ethan began talking.

Noah nodded, smiled bigger, and dug into his locker.

I couldn't stand here and watch this. I turned and headed to my next class. One foot in front of the other. Not paying much attention to people shoving and jostling around me. I'd known it would be like this. But that didn't mean I needed to torture myself by watching.

I made a decision—yes, I'd help Ethan. But I wasn't going to watch the promposal; nor was I going to be his in-person romance coach. If I didn't have to see them together, it would be easier to treat this as a scientific project, a study. Something that didn't personally impact me.

I needed to remove my emotions from the equation. And to do that, I had to stop thinking of Noah and Ethan as real people.

But that didn't mean I liked it. In fact, I kind of wanted to punch myself in the face. Frustration simmered just beneath my skin. I needed to shake this off.

I dug my phone out, forced myself to make a wacky face, took a pic, and sent it to Camilla. I'd just fake it until I felt better.

Until the mental image of Ethan and Noah standing together didn't splinter my stupid heart into pieces.

CHAPTER ELEVEN

Camilla

I rubbed the tight spot on the back of my neck and peered down at my notes. Mrs. Brandwright talked about something, but I didn't pay much attention to what she was saying. I was too busy trying not to remember how Benjamin's mouth had felt on mine, our bodies pressed together. Had it really been just yesterday?

I'd never been kissed like that before. Had never felt so overwhelmed and heady, like my skull was filled with helium. And I'd felt sexy, too. The way his eyes had flashed the moment before he'd taken my mouth . . . I smothered a groan and doodled on the corner of my notebook to distract myself.

To make matters even more awkward, Benjamin had barely said a word to me when he came into class. Had just dropped into his seat, gave me a courtesy nod, then opened a book in his lap and read.

Did he regret what had happened? Sure seemed that way, given his actions. Which only made me even more stressed about the whole thing.

Oh, well. I was totally done angsting over this. It was one kiss, that was all. Something impulsive and shocking and unlikely to ever happen again, so I needed to stop obsessing.

Mrs. Brandwright told us to get back into our groups and work on going over our notes so we could complete the group reporting session of our project. Carter hadn't shown up to school today—I was not going to take the fall for his absence, so I would just note somewhere that he hadn't bothered to participate in the group research portion.

Benjamin spun his desk around to face me. Finally looked me in the eyes. I couldn't read the nuances of emotion in them, but I could tell he was feeling just as uncomfortable as I was.

I pushed down a swell of anxiety and put on my game face. Gave a big smile and said, "Ready to relive the fun of scaring innocent people?"

He chuckled, and the tension between us cracked away just a bit. "It was pretty epic."

We spent a few minutes reviewing our notes in silence. The other groups around us hummed with light conversation. I heard Benjamin bark a laugh and looked up.

"Just saw my notes on when you tried to hold that old man's hand and then he wouldn't let yours go after you tried to walk away."

"Yeah, I wasn't sure I was ever going to get my hand back." That poor old guy had clung to me like I was a long-lost child or something. In a way, it made me sad that he was so starved for affection, he'd take it from a stranger. I made a mental note to try smiling more at old people.

Benjamin's eyes twinkled. "Have to admit, it was a lot of fun watching you relax and get into the project. You seemed pretty nervous at first. Did you find it challenging to get past your fear?"

"Are you kidding?" I laughed. "I was brought up to be polite to strangers, to stay quiet and not disrupt others. Forcing myself into their presence in such strong ways was super hard."

He nodded. "Same. But the fighting was the hardest part for me. I knew it was fake, but I still got caught up in it a couple of times."

"Me too. I even found my body starting to do the fight-or-flight response."

Thinking of our fake fights made me think of . . . I saw his gaze drop down to my mouth for a split second. The pulse in my throat stuttered. I knew what he was thinking about right now, could tell by the way his pupils flared.

Sure didn't look like regret in his eyes right now.

My lips parted on their own, and I swallowed. Drew in a steadying breath and tried to focus on something else. "Um. So, reading anything good?" I asked with a nod toward the thin paperback in his lap.

"*The Outsiders*," he said as he held it up.

"Oh, cool. I read that one. 'Stay gold, Ponyboy,'" I quipped.

He gave me a crooked smile, and my heart flipped in my chest. "This is one of my favorite books."

"What makes you like reading so much?" I mean, I liked books too, but Benjamin seemed to devour them like they were oxygen.

He paused, lips pressed as he thought. "I enjoy diving into other worlds, I guess. I like experiencing life through someone else's point of view. I like books that challenge me—banned books, edgy books, ones that make you stop and think."

Funny how talking about books made him open up more. A

smile crept along my face. "You make me want to run to the library right now."

"Schoolwork is overrated."

"I'll say."

There was another pause between us, but this one felt comfortable. Our shared smiles were easy and relaxed. Finally, Benjamin glanced down at his paper. Cleared his throat. "Well. Our conversations derail off-topic far too easily."

"Guess we should stop being so engaging." I grinned, and he did the same.

The bell rang.

"Okay, folks," Mrs. Brandwright called out over the sound of people gathering their stuff to run out of class. "Make sure you guys find time outside of class to wrap up your discussions, please. I'll see you tomorrow."

Neither Benjamin nor I moved. Just sat in place as the room emptied around us.

"We should finish this soon," I said.

"Yes."

"When are you free?" My heart began to beat hard against my rib cage.

"Tonight?"

"Sure. Yeah. Let's do that. Then we can get it done." Gah, I couldn't stop my bobblehead nodding or verbal vomiting.

He gave me that sexy crooked grin as he stood, and my heart raced harder. "I'll call you later to finalize details."

We gathered our stuff and headed out of class. It felt like my body was homed to him; I was aware of how far behind me he stood, the soft rasps of his breath. My cheeks burned, and my hands trembled.

I practically ran to my locker, then flicked it open and stuck my head inside. *Knock it off,* I ordered myself. *Stop being such a doofus around him.* I dragged in a few slow breaths, then withdrew my head and gathered my stuff.

Now to go home, finish my homework, and find the perfect casual outfit that screams "sexy" but doesn't try too hard. Yeah, no biggie.

"What toppings do you like?" I asked Benjamin.

He shrugged. "I'm not picky."

The crown of his dark blond hair glowed in the soft light of the pizza place where we sat, notebooks spread across the table. We'd decided to snag a bite to eat and finish our group reporting at the same time. I knew it wasn't a date—of course not. It was basically an extension of our classroom.

But it sure seemed like a date on the outside. From the intimate glow of the small pendant light above us, to being seated at the quiet table back in the corner, to the way both of us had changed from our school outfits into something fresh. This didn't look like just another school project.

Neither of us had thought to ask Carter if he wanted to meet either. Of course, after griping about him so much, I felt bad that maybe he was sick, which would explain his absence. Still, he needed to work that out with Mrs. Brandwright; we couldn't put everything on hold, wondering where he was.

I nibbled on my thumbnail. Stared at the extensive menu. "Do you like traditional pizza more, or are you open to trying something else? This barbeque chicken pizza sounds really good."

"Let's do that." He closed his menu, waved at the nearby

waitress, and placed our order. Then he turned his attention back to our notes. "Okay, so we have our results broken down by age and gender now. Is there anything else we're forgetting?"

I flipped through my pages. "I don't think so."

"Then let's go ahead and start drafting the group portion of the report."

For the next twenty minutes, we spent a lot of back-and-forth time refining our introductory paragraphs. I wrote hasty notes down as we haggled about word choice here and there. Still, it went rather smoothly.

The pizza arrived on a large round silver tray. I shoved my notes to the side and pressed a hand to my stomach. "I'm starving."

It tasted even better than I'd thought it would, which made it really hard to take my time and eat slowly, like a lady, instead of inhaling three slices and freaking him out with my appetite. Joshua called me a vacuum. He was just jealous of my metabolism.

We ate and talked more, both of us focused on getting the paragraphs written. I rubbed my fingers on my napkin when I saw a couple of small grease stains on the paper. "Don't worry," I said with a laugh. "I'll have clean hands when I type and print this out for us." We'd decided I'd type the intro and he'd make the corresponding charts.

"Not worried at all," he replied smoothly.

When the last sentence was done, I dropped my pencil and held my hands over my head. "Victory!" Done on time. Pretty good for me. I gave myself a congratulatory pat on the back, then grabbed another slice.

I heard a soft giggle a couple of tables away and saw a teen couple leaning toward each other, hands held over the table. The guy lifted her hand and pressed a kiss to her knuckles, and her cheeks got a pretty pink flush.

Benjamin glanced over at them, and his face flashed an emotion I couldn't place. "Monday isn't a typical date night," he finally said.

I gave a nervous laugh. "No, I suppose not."

He sipped his water. "What's the worst date you've ever been on?"

I bit my lip and pondered the question. I hadn't been on a lot of dates, to be honest. But I didn't want to look lame, so I dug through my brain for the one that was the worst. "Well, last year this guy asked me out to a really nice restaurant. Then 'forgot' his wallet at home. I didn't have enough money to cover it, so I had to call my dad to bail us out."

"Wow." He cringed. "That's pretty bad."

"Yeah. Needless to say, it was also our last date." The saddest part was, the guy didn't seem to even care that he'd been a total douche. He still waved at me in the hallways sometimes. I just shook my head. "But Joshua has an even better one. He went on a date with a guy who showed up dressed just like him, down to hairstyle and shoes. Even talked like him. It was so creepy that Joshua faked stomach cramps about ten minutes in and bailed."

Benjamin laughed. "That's a first."

"How about you?"

"I've been lucky to not really have had any bad dates."

I wasn't sure what to say to that, so I just nodded.

He chewed on his lower lip and shot me a surprisingly shy look. "Actually, I haven't been on a lot of dates at all. In case you haven't noticed, I'm rather awkward."

My chest swelled; Benjamin was opening up to me. I reached

over and patted his hand in what was supposed to be a friendly gesture, but once my fingers touched his, I found myself stroking them. Just once, just to touch his skin.

He flipped his hand over and, with his index finger, stroked my palm. A smooth slide that sent shivers dancing across my flesh. My lips parted, and his eyes grew dark and hooded.

"Here's your check," the waitress said, and we jerked away from each other, the mood broken. My cheeks burned, and I tried to recover by digging into my purse while she walked away.

"I got it," Benjamin said.

"No, it's okay. I—"

"Seriously. It's fine." The quiet firmness in his voice drew my attention. I peered into his eyes and saw flickers in his pupils. "I can pay for pizza, Camilla."

I gave a hesitant nod and put my wallet away. "That's really sweet of you. Thanks."

"It's not."

"What?"

Benjamin leaned forward. His face was lean and shadowed because of the dim light above us, and his eyes were all intensity, locked on mine. "I'm not a sweet guy. I'm abrupt. People say I'm off-putting. But you keep trying to talk to me anyway. Why?"

There was so much genuine questioning in his eyes that I couldn't look away. "Why? Because I think you're interesting," I admitted. I dropped my hands in my lap so I wouldn't be tempted to brush my fingers along his hair. "You see the world in a way I don't. You're quiet, yes, but there's a depth to you that isn't in most guys in our school."

I was drawn to Benjamin. And the more he dropped those

walls and let me in, the more he revealed these surprising snippets about himself, the more I wanted to get closer. To taste that mouth again, to let this raging emotion in my chest burst free.

But he was so hard to read, and I was afraid. One minute it seemed like he liked me. The next, he was pushing me away. Was he just too afraid to rush into it, given the confession about not dating a lot? Or was he still sorting out how he felt?

"I think you're interesting too." His words were quiet, but they stirred something in my soul.

Benjamin found me interesting. Perhaps there was hope after all.

CHAPTER TWELVE

Joshua

This cheeseburger makes me happy to be alive." Ethan took a huge bite of his burger, a blissful smile on his face as he chewed.

I nodded, then polished off the last bite of mine. "It was cooked perfectly." The guys at Rustic Burgers didn't joke around with hamburgers. There weren't a ton of fancy toppings, no gourmet offerings. What you got were amazing, regular burgers for dirt cheap. No wonder so many high schoolers hung out here.

For a Wednesday-night crowd, it was pretty packed. Ethan and I were sitting at a small table near the middle of the room, surrounded by a huge group of jocks who were laughing and shoving burgers into their faces.

Ethan put his burger down and snagged a fry from the overfilled basket we were sharing. "Okay. Ideas. Let's start brainstorming."

I made myself snag a fry and casually eat it. The moment I'd been dreading. I reminded myself to think of it as a project, nothing more. Nothing personal. "I need to know more about him first. Did you do your research?"

He nodded and dug out a folded piece of paper from his back pocket. Smoothed it on the table. "Here's what I found. Noah has three younger sisters. He likes science and acting. Enjoys most pop music, though he prefers electronica." He stopped to draw in a quick breath, eyes scanning the page. "He prefers khakis over jeans. He's a vegetarian—"

"You're in love with a vegetarian?" I blurted out.

Ethan blinked. "I, uh, what?"

Shit. Hadn't meant to say that out loud. But I was a little surprised by that—Ethan loved red meat like *whoa*. I waved my hand. "Nothing. Go on."

He looked at me for a long beat, then turned his attention back to the paper. "That's about it. It's not a lot, is it?" His mouth turned down and his eyes dimmed.

"Hey, it gives us somewhere to start," I rushed to say. "We'll make it work. Okay, so music and science and acting are strong interests. Sounds like you might want to dress up a bit to do this."

"Oh! Yes, probably not in a tux," Ethan said with a chuckle. A subtle reference to poor Camilla's promposal. "But dressed nicely. Maybe you could compose a song I could sing to him?"

My lungs seized, and my face froze.

Luckily, Ethan didn't notice my reaction. "Nah, that's not quite right," he continued. Rubbed his brow for a moment, deep in thought. "I wonder if I could get the school in on something. Like a fake scene from a musical? Maybe the theater teacher could help." He ate a handful of fries and kept talking. "Or I could take him to a concert and get the DJ to play something special for him."

"I think—"

"We could go to the amusement park and sit at the top of the

Ferris wheel, and when we looked down, there could be people spelling out the word 'prom' with their bodies!"

Oh, wow. Okay, this was getting a bit crazy. "Maybe—"

"No, no, wait! I could hire a skywriter to spell it out. We'd just need to make sure it's a clear day, and I could get him to stand outside on the front lawn—"

"Ethan!" I said in a loud almost-yell. "I think you need to scale it back a bit."

He blinked at me, and I saw the near-manic edge to his face ease up. "A little too over the top, huh?"

"Just a touch." I snagged a fry. "It's not about how big it is."

He snorted.

I slit my eyes and waved the fry at him. "Dirty boy. You know what I mean."

"I do. Please, go on." He planted his hands in his lap and focused those brilliant eyes on me.

I swallowed. Attempted to find my train of thought. Oh, right. "Um, it's not about how massive the *gesture* is. It's about the heart that's behind it. Not cheese, not desperation." I raised a brow and gave him a knowing look. "It's about sincerity. Sentimentality. The best approach is to make him feel special, make him unable to say no because he's so overwhelmed—in a good way."

"What do you think's the best promposal?"

I sucked in a loud breath. Frowned. No way could I go down this road with him. It was bad enough I was helping to hook him up with someone else.

"No, really. Please. I suck at this. But I trust you and your opinion, and I need your help. Please." His eyes begged me. "What do you feel would be the ultimate promposal?"

I took a long drag from my straw. Debated the question for a good minute. Because I knew it would kill me to see my ideal promposal used on someone else. But I also had some crazy, masochistic urge to confess to him how I felt. Maybe this would appease that need without giving too much away and hurting our friendship.

He didn't have to know that it would be my ideal promposal from him.

"Well," I started to say as I leaned back in my chair. "The best promposal is the one that comes from the heart. It doesn't try too hard. It's confident without being arrogant or fake. It shows that you understand the person, have taken the time to pay attention and learn him. Nothing is more flattering than feeling like someone gets you."

He nodded, a tiny encouragement for me to continue.

I dropped my attention to the table and gathered my courage. "My ideal promposal would be simple, but done in stages. First, I'd get a mix CD sent to my house, and the songs on it would all have special meaning. Maybe I'd get flowers the next day—something living, not cut. I want a plant I can grow. Symbolic of how he and I would grow together. And the following day I'd get something that showed us connected, like pictures we'd taken together. It would make me laugh and smile as I thought about how much fun we always had."

My throat tightened, and I thought about the corkboard in my bedroom that was covered with pictures of me, Ethan, and Camilla. And the ones hidden in a small photo album in my top dresser drawer that were just me and him. I clenched my hands. I didn't dare look up now. So much of my personal emotions were spilling into my words, and I couldn't quite hold them all back.

I made myself continue. "On the day of the promposal, it wouldn't happen in front of people—there would be no big public display. Because the show isn't what matters. It would be just the two of us, standing under a big blue sky, the sun shining down on our faces." If I closed my eyes, I could see me and Ethan, standing like that. Hands linked together, mouths turned up in smiles. I knew his face so well, I saw every detail in my dreams. "And . . . the guy would tell me how this wasn't just about prom. It was about us, our friendship, the start of our future. It would be quiet and simple and romantic, and . . ." I stopped myself and finally risked a look at Ethan.

Emotion poured out of his large eyes. His mouth was a thin line, and he just stared at me. No words.

I stared back. Silence pulsed between us, a living entity.

He swallowed, blinked. Stood. "I need to go to the bathroom." And then rushed away from the table.

Shit, shit, shit. I wanted to bang my head on the table in frustration; all my muscles were clenched in agonizing tension. I'd given myself away, and Ethan had freaked out. Of course. Because what was supposed to be a detached conversation had turned intimate, personal. Had revealed things about me we'd never discussed before.

I scrubbed a hand over my face and shoved the basket of fries away. My stomach had turned, was cramped and hurting a little. *Relax,* I told myself. I hadn't specifically mentioned his name. Surely he wouldn't figure it out from that.

But beneath that tension and stress was a thick layer of hurt. Because even though Ethan wouldn't know it was about him, something in him had rejected my vision. Had run away from it.

My chest burned, and my eyes stung. I blinked. No way in hell was I going to cry right now. No. Way. In. Hell.

I dug out my phone and shot Camilla a text. *Blew it—freaked Ethan out. Talked about promposal. Told him my perfect one. Think I admitted too much. What do I do??*

My fingers shook as I hit send.

A moment later, the phone buzzed back. *Hugs—STAY COOL. We'll talk l8r, k? Keep chin up. Be your charming self. <3*

She was right. I needed to fake my way through the rest of this evening. Then I could go home and analyze this conversation to death. But for now, smile, smile, smile.

I lifted my shoulders, lifted my chin, made myself eat a French fry, then another. Like nothing in the world was bothering me.

After a minute, Ethan came back. He gave me a chagrined grimace. "Hey, I'm sorry. I just . . . I don't know what happened."

"It's fine," I said with an airy wave of my hand. I was back in control of myself. "I got a little *verklempt* myself. So, back to the subject. Let's iron out what you're going to do."

He paused. "Maybe we can do this another day."

"Don't be ridiculous." I scoffed. "We're running out of time. We need to start firming up your plans now, or it isn't going to happen." I was proud that none of the fleeting hope I felt at that thought came through on my face or in my words.

"Are you sure?" He seemed hesitant.

I pointed at my face and gave him a charming smile. "Is this the face of a guy who's unsure?"

Rather than make him laugh, his frown deepened. "You don't need to do that, you know."

"Do what?"

"Act like things didn't get weird."

"Everything is fine." I widened my smile. Ate another French fry. "Okay. What was weird was me getting oddly sentimental in such a public place. But now you know what to tell all my secret admirers if they want to know the best way to ask me to prom."

He thinned his lips, and an emotion flickered across his face too fast for me to identify it. "Who are you going with, by the way? I just realized that in all this fuss over me, we haven't talked about *your* plans."

That stopped me. I hadn't thought up a plausible lie to feed him on what I was going to do. Mostly because I figured he'd be so distracted by trying to win Noah that he wouldn't think about me. Pride made me lie through my teeth. "There's . . . a guy I'm going to ask."

He raised an eyebrow. "Who?"

"He's not someone you know."

"I know a lot of people. Who is it?"

"He doesn't go to our school," I fudged.

"Where did you two meet?"

I swallowed. "At . . . the mall." Okay, I really sucked at this lying thing. "So, what do you think you're going to do about the promposal?"

Ethan leaned forward, relentlessly pushing. "And when did you meet him?"

"A few months ago or something. We're just casual friends."

"Why didn't you bring him up before, then?"

"Why? Are you jealous?" The words shot out of my mouth before I could stop them.

He huffed and leaned back in his chair. Crossed his arms over his chest. "Jealous? No. You're my best friend. No one can take that away from me."

If I didn't know better, I'd suspect he *was* jealous. But I did know better, and Ethan wasn't the type. If anything, he was probably hurt I hadn't mentioned the guy. And now I'd dug myself into it so deeply that I had to come up with a backstory on someone who didn't even exist.

"I'm not even sure I'm going to ask him," I said in a firm tone. "I'm still ironing out my plans." Which now included begging Camilla to help me dig my way out of this ridiculous hole. "So for now, I'd rather we spend the time focused on you and your issue. One problem at a time, okay?"

His nod wasn't convincing. "You know we can talk about anything, right?" he asked me.

"Of course I do. And when I have something I need to discuss, I'll bring it up. I promise." Fake guys and secret loves didn't count as things I needed to discuss. At least, not with him. "Our fries are getting cold, and my ass is getting numb sitting in this seat."

He sighed but acquiesced. "Fine, princess. Let's finish up here so you can massage those glutes."

The next half hour was a bit rough, but eventually Ethan relaxed and seemed to let go of our previous discussion. He decided his promposal shouldn't be too flashy, though it was still up in the air whether or not it would be in front of others. He was also torn on which angle to take—if he should make it music-themed or theater-themed. I encouraged him to take a couple of days to mull it over and we'd refine the plan then. Mostly because at that point, I wanted to just get the hell out of there.

As I walked home, I couldn't believe I'd done that. Lied to Ethan, right to his face. I couldn't remember the last time I'd fibbed like that. Probably the candy bar debacle in eighth grade, when I'd made him think Camilla had eaten his Milky Way when it was really me. But guilt had made me fess up to it shortly after.

I dug out my phone and walked on the mostly empty sidewalk, darkness cocooning me. Then I dialed the one person who could help me now.

"Hey, you okay?" Camilla sounded concerned.

I sucked in a steady breath and exhaled. "I did something super dumb."

"Wouldn't be the first time."

"Hardy har." I turned right and kept going down the sidewalk until I was on her doorstep. "I'm outside. I hope you have sugar products, because I'm about to destroy them all."

I heard footsteps pounding inside. Then the door flung open. Camilla stood there in baggy sweatpants and a tank top. She wrapped me in a big hug.

"Come in, come in," she soothed as she ushered me into the house. "There's nothing some chocolate chip cookies and your female bestie can't fix."

CHAPTER THIRTEEN

Camilla

Ugh. For whatever reason, this Thursday was the slowest day in the history of slow days. First period felt like it lasted twelve hours. By the time I got to psych, my last class for the day, I was dragging ass.

I plopped into my seat, and Benjamin glanced at me over his shoulder.

"Late night?" he commented with an eyebrow raised.

My lips twitched, and a little bit of life infused in me. "Not really." Though I had stayed up a little later than usual working on my solo portion of our group project, where we evaluate each other and discuss our overall thoughts, how we felt the project personally impacted us, et cetera.

"Class, we have a lot of information to get through today, and I also want to allow you time to finish up your projects." Mrs. Brandwright perched on the edge of her desk, and the class noise settled to quiet. "I hope you've made good progress, because they're due tomorrow."

There were a few stifled groans around us. I heard Carter

sigh from behind me. Mrs. Brandwright had pulled us aside and mentioned Carter would be doing his own project, due to missing school for the last several days from illness. So we didn't need to include him in our work. I was glad he was feeling better but also a bit relieved we weren't dependent on him anymore.

She began to give her lecture, and I dutifully wrote notes. We were wrapping up our discussion of social mores, and I had to admit, I was curious what would be next. Were there more group projects in our future? Could I possibly be paired with Benjamin again? No, there hadn't been another kiss. But we'd been talking every day this week, passing notes, discussing books and music and art.

There was a tap on my knee. My heart did that painful, excited thud it always did when he passed me a note. I dropped my hand down and grabbed it, unfolded it.

What book made you uncomfortable to read as a kid?

I bit my lower lip to keep from giggling out loud at the first one that popped into my mind. But I couldn't hide my smirk as I scrawled, *Are You There God? It's Me, Margaret* on the paper. Then added, *It was accompanied by* The Talk, *along with an awkward demonstration on pads.*

I handed it back to him. Paper rustled. I heard him laugh, which he covered quickly with a cough. My grin widened.

The note was passed back.

Sounds like there's a story in there. My mom drew pictures as well when I got The Talk. *Also checked out books on anatomy. It was scarring.*

I chewed on the end of my pen. As I tried to come up with something witty to reply, my phone buzzed. I dug it out of my pocket.

Roses, right? But do you have a color preference? It's for the corsage.

I should be happy that my prom date was so attentive to my needs. But it felt like an interruption. The impossible had happened: Benjamin was talking to me now, opening up to me like we were friends . . . with the real potential to grow into more. Not to mention that Zach had stopped hounding me for a couple of days.

Apparently not for good, though.

Doesn't matter to me, I typed back, then sent.

My phone buzzed a moment later. I closed my eyes and drew in a steadying breath so I didn't write something rude. But the message wasn't from Zach.

So who is this mystery guy Joshua likes?

A text from Ethan. Interesting. He wasn't a texting kind of guy. Could he be jealous, even if he didn't know it? I gnawed on my lip, trying to figure out the best strategy to take.

Don't know much about him, tbh, I finally replied. *But if Joshua likes him, he's probably awesome.* I was proud of myself when I hit send. The message was a subtle compliment to Ethan, though of course he didn't have a clue about that. But it also increased the intrigue around Joshua and his mysterious "guy."

I stuck my phone back in my pocket and pretended to pay attention for another few minutes. Wrote a couple of halfhearted notes in my notebook so I wouldn't feel completely lost when trying to study later. Then turned my focus back on the note Benjamin had written.

Life takes strange turns sometimes, doesn't it? I paused in my writing. Thought about what I really wanted to say. Maybe Benjamin would have a good perspective on the Ethan-Joshua situation.

I have a friend who's in love with someone. They're really close. But the person has no idea how my friend feels. I don't know how to help.

I waited impatiently for his response.

"Okay. Use this last chunk of time to wrap up your project," our teacher said. "Solo work from now until the bell."

A moment later, the tap on my knee let me know I had a reply.

Sometimes there are reasons people stay silent about feelings. Does your friend have one? Will this ruin their friendship or hurt another person?

Hmm. Good questions. Who would get hurt by Joshua telling Ethan how he felt? Well, Joshua, of course, if Ethan rejected him. It would probably mess up their friendship, too. Ethan and I weren't as close as they were, though I adored the guy. We both basically shared Joshua as best friend. As weird as it sounded, it worked for us.

That said, if he hurt Joshua, it might change my feelings about him. It would be hard not to resent him to some degree for causing that pain.

So much at stake here. Maybe my text to Ethan was a bit rash. Maybe I shouldn't get involved. After all, if my actions caused things to fall apart for them, I'd feel horrible.

It's a complicated situation, I replied to Benjamin. *My friend is still trying to sort it out. I just hate feeling powerless.*☹

I paused and looked at his words again. It was strange, talking to him like this. Normally, Joshua was my sole confidant for the big things. But something about Benjamin inspired confidence. His thoughtful demeanor, the way he challenged me to look at things from a different point of view.

I trusted him.

Wow.

I wanted to keep talking to him. To open up and let him know how I felt . . . to see if he might possibly feel the same about me too. But I was scared.

Like Joshua, I had my own reasons for staying quiet and not confessing my true feelings. Rejection was a powerful deterrent. Plus, I wasn't fully confident in the signs he was throwing me. I felt like we were becoming friends. But could he ever want more than that? I wanted his friendship, *and* I wanted more.

I appreciate you talking to me about this, I continued writing. *I guess we'll see what fate has in store.*

A good answer for not only Joshua's situation, but mine.

The final bell rang a minute after I handed him the note. We both lingered at our desks while the class emptied out, our typical practice over the last few days. I gave him a shy smile, which he returned.

We finally gathered our stuff.

"I'll see you tomorrow," I said.

He nodded.

"You nervous about our project?"

"Nope. I think we did fine."

"Me too. But still, I always get nervous. For any project, not just ones in this class, I mean." I was prolonging our good-bye. Babbling like an idiot. *Stop it.* "Anyway. Okay. See ya."

He turned to the left, and I went to my locker. Got my stuff. Kept my attention firmly on my own belongings instead of watching him walk away. That boy was mixing me up in the head. I was normally pretty good at reading people, but he was an enigma.

I met Joshua just inside the double doors, and we headed out into the sunshine. The weather was warming up, and it felt good not to have to bundle up like crazy, though there were slushy puddles everywhere.

I quickly recapped my conversation with Ethan and showed him the two texts—Ethan hadn't replied to my response.

Joshua frowned. "What does this mean?"

"I'm not sure. Either he's starting to realize he might have feelings for you, or he's upset that he was left out of the conversation about this guy."

"Who doesn't even exist."

"He doesn't know that." I peered up at the pale blue sky, streaked with thin strips of clouds. "Your impulse told you to make him up. Obviously, you wanted Ethan to start seeing you as a person desired by others. It really wasn't a bad idea. Kinda wish I'd thought of it myself."

He elbowed me with a laugh. "You come up with enough good schemes on your own. I just learned by watching you."

"So, are you guys okay? You and Ethan, I mean."

He shoved his hands in his jeans pockets. Shrugged. His eyes were hooded, though I saw a twinge of pain there. "It's weird. Ethan's acting like nothing happened. He's been all smiles, though a little more keyed up than usual. I can't figure him out."

"The promposal is on Monday, right? Maybe he's nervous about it. Not to mention the fact that he might be feeling left out about you liking someone. That probably hurt his feelings." God, this was so crazy complicated. No wonder Joshua felt like he was in over his head.

"I wasn't trying to hurt him." He raked a hand through his

dark hair, leaving small spikes all over the top. Frustration dug a deep line between his brows. "I just . . . I don't know how much longer I can keep going like this. Pretending we're friends when all I want to do is grab him by the shirt and kiss him senseless."

I thought about Benjamin's eyes, his mouth on mine. I hadn't told anyone about our kiss, afraid of what they'd tell me. I knew Joshua would kick my ass when he eventually found out—and he would. But I was still trying to make sense of it all. "I totally know what you mean." God, this sucked. We both needed to think about something else before we imploded. "Anyway. Tell me more about your plans for the summer. You're going right to New York City after we graduate, right?" I slugged him in the arm in an effort to mask my sudden burning tears. "Jerk. I'm going to miss you."

He rubbed his arm and shot me a glare. "There's no need for violence just because you're jealous of my life."

"Sorry, sorry." I gave him a cheeky grin and sniffled back my tears.

Part of my brain couldn't accept that he was going to be gone in a couple of months. That I'd see him only at winter and summer breaks. We'd been so close for so long now, practically glued at the hips, as our parents joked. At least I knew he'd stay in touch—both of us already had Skype accounts set up so we could chat in our dorm rooms. Still, it wouldn't be the same.

"You know I'm terribly jealous," I admitted. "You're going to have so much fun and independence. If I moved that far away from here, I'm pretty sure my mom would pack up our house and follow me."

Joshua chuckled. "Yeah, she probably would. Luckily, my dad

is pretty set on staying here. I have an aunt who lives just outside the big city, and I'm going to stay with her and work on finding a job before the semester starts."

"Doing what?"

"Whatever it takes to earn money."

"Don't sell crack."

He wrinkled his nose. "Crack is so old-school. I'm strictly a pills guy."

"Funny." I shoved him with my shoulder. "So you'll stay there—"

Joshua stopped me in place and put a finger over his mouth. I shut up quickly and looked in the direction he was pointing.

There sat Dwayne and Niecey, on a bench that faced away from us. He had a bouquet of wildflowers in his hand, which he handed to her. From her profile, I could see she was smiling.

We slowed our pace to a crawl until we were close enough to hear them.

"—love you, Niecey," he was saying. He drew a finger along the curve of her cheek and stared into her gorgeous brown eyes.

Her smile widened, and she leaned into his touch. "I love you too. And these flowers are beautiful. Thank you."

"I thought for a long time about what would be the perfect promposal for you," he said. "I even thought about doing something in front of the school. But everyone there already knows how beautiful and amazing you are, and I wanted this to be about us."

I practically melted into a puddle on the spot. I heard Joshua give a soft sigh too, and I knew he was just as impacted as I was.

Dwayne leaned over, brushed a kiss against Niecey's lips. "I want to take you to prom. Show you off on my arm as the most gorgeous girl in that room. Treat you like a princess, the way you deserve. Will you go to prom with me?"

My heart fluttered wildly. Hell, I was so swoony at this point that I almost shouted yes for her.

Niecey beamed at him, pressed small kisses to his face, his lips. "Yes. I will. I love you."

Dwayne pumped a fist in the air. "Yes! Nailed it!" he said with a wink and then leaned toward her mouth.

They started making out, and Joshua and I mutually decided we didn't want to witness that part. We slipped past them and kept heading toward our houses.

Neither one of us spoke for a couple of minutes. Then I said, "That was the sweetest promposal I've ever seen."

He nodded. "It was perfect. He did it exactly right. Made it about her, not about the spectacle."

How would Benjamin ask a girl to prom? He'd said he wasn't sure if he was going. But did he like anyone?

No matter how much he and I were starting to connect, I wasn't going to get that sort of gesture from him. I was already committed to another guy.

"You okay?" Joshua asked me.

I shrugged. "Just . . . thinking."

"I know. Me too."

My heart pinched. Poor guy. Monday was going to be terrible for him. Watching the guy he loved do something beautiful and emotional for another person. I reached over and took his hand. Squeezed it. "Hey, tell me more about New York. What you're going to do while you're there."

He shot me a grateful but sad smile. I knew he saw right through me, knew I was trying to distract him. But he appreciated it anyway. "I'm planning to watch every Broadway production I can afford, of course. Stay up all night and walk the city streets. Maybe even bust out my old film camera and take pictures."

Yes, there would be miles separating us far too soon. But we were stronger than that.

CHAPTER FOURTEEN

Joshua

Friday morning, I sat down in my seat and warmed up my trumpet. Other instruments chimed in around me, adding to the cacophony of noise filling the band room. I did a couple of scales up and down, up and down.

Tyler, my stand mate and fellow first trumpet, dashed over and whipped his trumpet out of his case. He did a few halfhearted blows through the mouthpiece, blue eyes scanning the room the whole time.

"Everything okay?" I asked him.

"Yeah. Fine." He blew out a few more notes. Emptied the spit valve.

"Uh-huh, sure." I flipped to the current piece we'd been working on and practiced the notes with just my fingers, tapping away at the buttons. This song had a few hard runs in it, and while I was pretty dexterous from playing guitar, I needed to improve my speed and accuracy.

More students filtered in; more noise filled the room. The

percussion section joined in, clanging and drumming and chiming away.

After a minute, Tyler stood and rested his trumpet on his seat. He shot me a cocky grin. "Finally, she's here. Been waiting to talk to her since lunch."

Ah, should have known. Tyler and Madison, his girlfriend since eighth grade, were pretty much inseparable. The two of them were probably going to get married out of high school, have twenty-five kids, and live on a riverboat. Sightings of them apart were pretty rare.

She waved at him, and he walked over to the flute section at the front of the room. "Hey, honey bunny." She pressed a sweet kiss to his cheek. "Sorry I was late."

He tucked a strand of red hair behind her ear. "Where were you?"

"Potty break. Couldn't hold it in."

"Ah. Well, you do have a tiny bladder."

She shot him a mock glare but laughed.

"So, I was thinking for prom, we could go to that new seafood place down the street from my house. My dad said it's great and he knows the chef, so he can get us a good table."

She lifted her chin and crossed her arms to peer at him over her nose, despite being a good six inches shorter than he was. There was a tight smile on her face, one that didn't meet her eyes. "Prom? What's all this about prom?"

Oh, shit. I saw what was about to happen. Obviously, he hadn't officially asked her, and she was calling him out on it. I stood to go warn Tyler, but a freshman who played second trumpet came over and asked me to show him how to do a high C.

By the time the kid left, Tyler and Madison were surrounded by several other practicing students in the flute section, and I couldn't hear what they were saying very well over the trills.

"—not going to ask me?" Madison cried out, her voice piercing the noise. The entire band room went quiet.

"Mad, this *is* me asking." Tyler rolled his eyes. "Seriously, you're doing this? You're going to fight with me over this? Right in the middle of the band room?"

Madison's cheeks burned. She drew in a loud breath through her nose. "Seriously, *you're* doing *this*? This bullshit is my promposal, for real? Where the hell are the flowers and the candy and the music and the romance? You effing ask me to prom *right in the middle of the band room*, just like that?"

A couple of people oohed. They shut up when Madison shot them a hot glare.

Tyler's jaw clenched, and he mirrored Madison's hostile stance, arms crossed in front of his chest. "We've been dating five years now. Do you mean to tell me it wasn't obvious we'd be going to prom together? That I really had to take a risk and ask you in such a ridiculous, overblown way?"

I shook my head and cringed. This was not going to end well.

Madison grew deathly still. Her face froze. She didn't say anything for a full minute, like she was trying to get herself under control, and all I could hear were the whispers of the guys in the percussion section. "What's obvious to me is that you're completely clueless. You've taken me for granted."

Tyler blinked and opened his mouth to speak, but Madison held up a hand and kept going.

"No, I don't want to hear anything else you have to say right now. I'm not doing this with you."

"Fine. We'll talk about it later," he shot back. "In *private*."

"No, we won't." She undid a gold necklace around her throat and tossed it in the air toward him. He just barely caught it before it hit the ground. "I mean I'm done. We're over." She blinked, and a tear rolled down her cheek. She swiped at it with a shaky hand. "I just can't believe you." With that parting shot, she grabbed her purse and her flute case and ran out the band room door.

"Wait. What the hell?" Tyler just stood there, dumbly watching Madison go.

A girl in the flute section, one of Madison's friends, shot him a hate-filled glare and ran after her.

The whispers kicked in again, layering furiously upon one another.

"—can't believe she just dumped him like that," one guy said with a harsh scoff. "Cold."

"Well, I can't believe he didn't bother to even ask her to prom," a girl replied in a hushed tone. "Seriously? That was the lamest promposal ever."

Tyler didn't move from his spot until the band director, Mrs. Wilders, came out of her office and headed toward the podium. She shooed him into his section.

Hunched over, he walked quietly to our row and sat down by my side. Stared at the music stand. "I can't believe that happened." He sounded angry and frustrated, his mouth thinned into a narrow line.

Mrs. Wilders tapped her baton on her massive music stand. "Scales, folks. Let's warm up."

The rest of band went by fast. Once the gossip died down and we got to work on our difficult piece, we were pretty productive.

But I could feel random stares hitting our section the entire time from all over. Everyone was looking at Tyler to see what he'd do, how he'd react to being dumped.

While Mrs. Wilders focused her attention on the clarinets, I patted Tyler on the shoulder. His muscles were so knotted I could feel them through his shirt. "Hey," I whispered. "You doing okay?"

He gave a stiff nod. "Fine."

"For what it's worth, I'm sorry." Underneath all that anger and frustration, I knew he was in a lot of pain. Embarrassed, too.

His jaw had a tic, and I saw him peek at the section where Madison and the other flute player were still missing. "I'll fix it."

"I know you will. If you need help, let me know."

For the first time since sitting down, he looked over at me. There was a hint of gratitude in his eyes, still mingled with the hurt. "Thanks. I will."

The bell rang, and we cleared out. Tyler was one of the first out of the classroom. Probably trying to find Madison and sort it all out.

I tucked away my trumpet case in the designated cubby and left the band room. Stopped by my locker to grab my lunch bag. As I did so, I saw Noah at his locker. His hair was artfully mussed and spiky, and he had on a pair of expensive jeans with a fitted navy blue shirt that showed off his muscles.

The guy was hot. I couldn't deny that. There was something about his self-confidence, his easygoing demeanor that drew people to him. No question why Ethan was so into him, at least physically. And yeah, he was nice, too. Probably helped little old ladies across the street and never cheated at Monopoly the way I did. But what else was there to him? What made my best guy friend willing to risk a public rejection to ask Noah to prom?

Only one way to find out.

I pushed back my shoulders and drew in a fortifying breath. Closed my locker and walked toward Noah like I was heading to the cafeteria. "Oh, hey," I told him as I neared him. "You're Noah, right?"

"Yup." He gave me a polite smile.

"I'm Joshua. I'm a friend of Ethan's."

The smile grew genuine. "Ethan, yeah. We have a class together." He closed his locker, and we both headed toward the cafeteria. "So, how do you know him? Are you guys good friends?"

Words flew out of my mouth before I could stop them. "Oh, he and I are *great* friends," I found myself saying with a smooth grin. "We've known each other since middle school."

His smile wobbled a touch. "Ah. I see."

My lungs squeezed with guilt, and I huffed a sigh. Crud, I couldn't do it. I could tell he was fishing, and my impulse was to play up my friendship. But I couldn't hurt Ethan like that. "You guys are in biology together, right?"

"Yeah. We are. He talked about me?" His cheeks flushed a touch.

This was for the best, I told myself. I was doing it for Ethan's happiness. "He did. All nice things too." I hoped he couldn't see the sadness in my eyes.

"Thanks." Noah nodded in appreciation at me. His eyes flared with hope. "Well, I'd better get going. Have a good one." He walked off, and I headed into the cafeteria, wishing I felt better about the nice thing I just did.

The promposal was going to happen on Monday. Yeah, there was no way in hell I could stick around and watch it. Maybe I could fake a sick day or leave after lunch or something. After all, Ethan would be too busy living out his dream to notice I wasn't around.

I saw Ethan sitting at the lunch table, talking to Camilla. And suddenly I just couldn't face him. My heart was crumbling apart in my chest. I couldn't sit there and fake like everything was okay. So I spun around and fled for the library. I shot Camilla a brief text explaining, then composed a text for Ethan that I would see him later—boy, it was so much easier to fake happiness when someone couldn't see my face.

A moment later, just as I settled into the back corner and sneak-opened my sandwich, my phone buzzed. A reply from Ethan. *Make sure you find time to eat!*

I shoved a piece of sandwich in my mouth and chewed. No worries about that, buddy. *BTW saw Noah in halls,* I replied. *Talked you up.* There. That should get me out of having to be present for the promposal on Monday.

It was a few minutes before I got a response. And when I did, all it said was *thx.*

You okay? I wrote back. A definite oddity for him to be so curt. *Fine. See ya later.*

Okay, then. I ate my sandwich, though it didn't taste great. I'd lost my appetite. Part of me was curious about why Ethan was so lackluster in his response about me talking to Noah. Did I do something wrong? Did he not want me to interfere at all?

That didn't seem like him.

Maybe he was just in a bad mood. It was rare, but it did happen.

The rest of my day went fast. I finished classes, walked home, then busted out my homework so I could focus on making dinner and relaxing.

I grabbed two thick tuna steaks out of the fridge and popped them in the skillet to sauté. As they finished cooking, I chopped veggies and steamed them. Cut two thick hunks of bread and made plates. "Dad, dinner's done."

He trudged out of the office, still wearing his pajama pants. His hair was a total mess. Even so, he was still an attractive man. I wondered if he'd ever start dating again. Wasn't quite sure how to broach that subject, though—we both avoided talking about dating in an unspoken agreement. "That smells amazing. I think you outdid yourself."

We took our plates to the table, and Dad grabbed a beer and cracked it open.

"How's the book?" I asked.

"Going great." He swigged the beer, then cut into the tuna. "This is perfect," he said around a mouthful. "Wow. If that music thing doesn't work out, you should go into cooking."

I chuckled. "Glad to see I have a fan."

"When you leave for New York, I'm gonna be living on peanut butter sandwiches," he teased.

"I don't doubt that at all. Guess I'll have to send you some care packages from school."

"So." Dad put his fork down and eyed me in earnest. "Son."

Aw, shit. I fought back a groan. Dad didn't bust out the "son" thing unless he was about to do some heavy talking. Which usually resulted in the two of us having an awkward conversation we both wanted out of after about three seconds.

"That time of the year again, is it?" I said in a droll tone.

He frowned. "It's serious, Joshua. We need to talk."

"About what?" Surely I hadn't done anything. I'd even turned in all my homework and had pulled up my grade in physics. No groundable offenses I could remember.

Dad cleared his throat, and his cheeks flushed. "I . . ." He tugged at the neckline of his T-shirt like it was strangling him. "So, I was wondering when you were going to tell Ethan you love him."

Holy crap. My dad couldn't have shocked me more than if he'd hit me upside the head with a brick. "You *know* about that?"

He barked a laugh. "Are you serious? I've known about your feelings for him for a long time. I've watched you help him with prom plans recently, and it makes me sad for you. Because I know you're pretending you don't care, to save his feelings." He ate some broccoli.

I pushed my food around on my plate. Where could I even start with this? "He likes someone else. I can't change that. And he's asking the guy on Monday. It's too late for me to have a chance."

He pursed his lips. "Kinda surprised you're not even trying."

I rubbed my brow. "I'm stuck, you know? He asked me for help."

"And did you help him?"

"Well . . . yeah." Ethan had finally decided on what he was going to do for his promposal. Not as quiet as I'd recommended, but still very personal, with music involved. Noah was sure to flip over it.

"So you did your part and you were a good friend. But friends don't keep secrets like this from each other. Don't you think he'll be hurt to know you've been hiding this from him for so long?"

I knew he was right. But that didn't change the fact that it would impact our relationship for good. I forced myself to finish my tuna steak. "But what if I tell him and he rejects me?"

Dad put his fork down and gave me a sad smile. "It's a risk, I know. But sometimes you have to take that gamble and try. I'm not going to push you into it, son. I just want you to be happy."

My throat closed up, so I just nodded my response. I knew Dad was right. But did I have the courage to tell Ethan, despite the odds being stacked against me?

Right now, I just didn't know.

CHAPTER FIFTEEN

Camilla

Mrs. Brandwright walked down the first aisle and handed back graded reports. As she made her way from person to person, my heart wouldn't stop racing. I'd worked so hard on my project.

When she reached our aisle, she paused in front of Benjamin first, then me. Her face was unreadable. My hand trembled a touch as I took the report from her.

A-minus.

Holy crap. Given what a hard-ass she was when it came to grading assignments, anything over a B-plus was rare.

I read her handwritten note at the top. *Wonderful job, Camilla. I'm so proud of the effort you and Benjamin put into this project. Great analysis, intriguing discussion topics, and good challenges, though I wonder if you couldn't have pushed yourself just a bit more out of your comfort zone. Other than that, well done. Kudos to you.*

I ripped off a piece of paper and wrote, *How was your grade?* Then I tapped Benjamin's left elbow.

He took the note and after a moment passed it back. *A-minus.*

I'll take it. Did you read anything good last weekend?

I grinned. He and I had been passing notes regularly every day for the last couple of weeks. I'd thought it would slow down or stop after our projects were turned in, but on the contrary, it had kept up.

No books, I wrote. *But I busted out my dad's record player and listened to some Pink Floyd. Do you like any of their music?*

Mrs. Brandwright moved to the front of the class and spent several minutes talking about our projects, which gave me a chance to keep talking to Benjamin. His note back to me said, *Their album* The Dark Side of the Moon *is a classic. My mom got me hooked on them. If you like their stuff, try listening to some old Genesis.*

"—did such a wonderful job, I want them to talk a little bit about what they did." Our teacher's smooth voice broke through, and I realized she'd stopped talking. A glance up confirmed she was staring right at me.

Crap.

I glued on a smile and shot Benjamin a desperate look.

Thankfully, the guy came to my rescue. He cleared his throat and started talking, and eventually I got caught up enough to jump in and add my own points. Then the spotlight turned off us, and she began to lecture.

Deciding I should probably pay attention so I didn't get busted for passing notes, I flipped my notebook open to a fresh page and jotted down key words and phrases. The period passed fast, and before I knew it, the last bell had rung.

Benjamin and I dawdled, as usual. We left the room side by side, walking at a comfortable pace down the hall.

"Thanks for bailing me out," I told him. "I was distracted."

"I can't imagine why," he replied with a straight face.

I should just do it. My pulse thrummed in excitement at the sudden thought. For days now, I'd been debating if I should ask Benjamin out. Not for a school project or as friends. But on a real date. Where we could talk outside of school, have food or see a movie, maybe even kiss again.

My lips tingled from remembered sensation, and it was hard not to press my fingers to my mouth.

I swallowed and steeled my courage. "So. Benjamin."

"So. Camilla." His eyes twinkled.

We stopped by his locker, and he got his belongings out.

"Um. I was thinking. That we should, y'know, we should hang out again. I mean, we can do anything, like catch a movie one night. Or get coffee. Or go to a bookstore, maybe." Oh my God. This was painful. My cheeks burned.

His hands stilled in his locker, and he kept his face turned away.

Shit. That wasn't a good response. My brain scrambled to back out. "But we don't have to if you're busy. I'm sure you're busy. It's—"

"I can't." His voice was so quiet I barely heard him.

"Oh."

He finally turned to look at me, and his eyes were filled with intensity. "I can't go out with you. I'm sorry. Zachary likes you way too much."

I blinked. "What? What does *he* have to do with this? He's my prom date, nothing else."

"He's my cousin."

My stomach sank clear to my feet. Of course he was. Because that was totally my luck. How did I not know about this before? I rubbed my brow and kept my attention on the tiled floor.

"Zachary has talked about you for months," he continued in a low voice. "It was hard for him to gather his courage to ask you out. I think he's hoping prom night will help you see a new, romantic side to him."

Ugh. God. Why did this have to happen to me? It wasn't enough that I was forced to go to prom with someone I didn't like. But now that had to impact something I might have with Benjamin? Not fair. "I see," I finally said, knowing my frustration was coming through my words.

He sighed and closed his locker door with a little more strength than was needed. "When he was asking for advice on his promposal, I didn't know at first that he meant you. And now I feel like an ass because of . . . well, you know." His gaze skittered away. "I didn't tell him about it."

The kiss. He did regret it, but not for the reasons I'd thought.

Oh, this sucked. So very much.

I drew myself up and made myself say, "Okay. Thanks for explaining." I turned and started walking away before I could do something else mortally embarrassing.

"Camilla," he said.

I turned.

His cheeks flushed a touch. "When he found out we were doing our school project together, he asked me to remember that he liked you first. He's my cousin—I can't hurt him like that."

My breathing shallowed, and I clenched my jaw and nodded. Fury washed over me, hot and fast. I spun around and left. Seriously, Zach called dibs on me because he decided we were going to have some great romance at prom? Even though he and

I had barely known each other before that—and even now, we'd hardly spoken?

What the hell?

I ripped my phone out of my pocket and banged out a message to him. *Where are you? We need to talk. Now.*

While I waited, I cleared my stuff out of my locker and sent Joshua a text that I'd be heading home later and would call him soon. My face burned; my chest ached with all the heated words I was biting back. I wanted to slam my head on the metal doors. Yeah, I understood now why Benjamin couldn't go out with me— you didn't make a move on someone your friend or relative liked.

But I'd never given Zach any impression that I was interested in him. He'd crossed a line.

My phone buzzed. *Everything okay?? I'm in the parking lot. Where should we meet?*

I'll be there in a minute.

I shoved the double doors open and stepped out into the warm sunshine. But the sun didn't make me feel better.

There were only a few cars in the lot, so it was easy to spot Zach standing by his dark blue car. I stomped up to him and struggled to keep myself from yelling in his face. Fresh anger filled my gut.

"Zach, do you realize we're going to prom as friends?"

He stiffened. "Um. Well, I—"

"We're *friends*, Zach. That's it. In fact, I said yes to your prom- posal because you asked me in front of everyone in school—and had it filmed, too. There was no way I could say no when you put me on the spot like that." I knew I was sounding super harsh, but I couldn't stop from spewing my wrath at him.

His eyes flashed with deep hurt, and he crammed his hands

in his jeans pockets. "Seriously? You only agreed because of how I asked you?"

My stomach turned at the pain on his face, and I felt a flash of guilt. I softened my next words. "I'm sorry. I didn't want to tell you like this, because I thought we could try to be friends and have a good time anyway. But . . . I can't pretend like it's going to be more, like it'll lead to us dating or something. If you want to go with someone else, a girl who might actually like you, I understand." Not that it would mend anything with me and Benjamin, who would still feel loyalty to his cousin. It appeared that boat had sailed, because of this guy right here and his sense of entitlement, despite *my* feelings on the matter.

His lips pursed, and his nostrils flared. "Whoa, are you dumping me?"

I bit back a frustrated growl. Leave it to him to twist what I was trying to tell him. "I'm saying—"

"Wait, wait, wait. Is there someone else you like?"

That got me to shut up. I couldn't exactly proclaim my feelings for his cousin. That would rub salt into the wound—and embarrass me, too. I was already kind of regretting being so harsh and blasting Zach like this. Yeah, he'd crossed a line with that little stunt he'd pulled, but that didn't mean I had to, as well.

His eyes narrowed. "There is, isn't there. Some other guy you want to go to prom with. And I have a feeling I know who."

I lifted my chin and stared down my nose. "That's not relevant to this conversation. This is about us." Kinda. Mostly.

"I should have seen this coming." Zach leaned back against his car and crossed his arms. "You've been avoiding me pretty much since I asked you to prom. I can't even get you to commit to a color."

"Seriously, that's not fair. You've been bombarding me with messages about it nonstop."

"Because prom isn't that far away!" He drew in a slow breath. "Have you gotten your dress, Camilla? Have you even gone shopping yet?"

I stared at him. He knew I hadn't—he could tell. And I suddenly felt very guilty. After all, I *had* said yes. But I'd been putting off shopping for a dress or for fabric because, well, it made it less real that way. "Well, I was planning to soon," I said, knowing I sounded super lame.

His voice was quiet as he said, "If I were Benjamin, you'd already have bought your dress."

And there it was. I shifted my bag on my shoulder. I was tempted to deny it, but what was the point? He'd find out soon enough that I'd asked Benjamin out on a date. "How did you know?"

He scoffed. "Seriously? Everyone in school knows. And I look like an idiot because I asked someone who is in love with someone else."

A twirl of panic threaded around my stomach and tightened. "What are you talking about, everyone?" How could people know? I hadn't done anything different lately. Yeah, we'd been talking and hanging out, but that could be blamed on our school project bringing us together.

Crap. Benjamin didn't know how I felt, did he? Was that the real reason he'd turned me down, because he didn't like me like that? Was he just using Zach as an excuse?

"Yes. He knows," he said in answer to my unspoken question, and all the air squeezed out of my lungs. His eyes flattened. "I overheard him talking with a few guys about how much you stare at him in your psychology class."

A wash of heat covered my cheeks, and I felt sick. Great. I was a joke.

But why had he kissed me?

Did that really matter? He'd already made it clear he didn't want to date me, regardless of the real reason.

"I never meant to lead you on," I finally told Zach. I was suddenly tired and just wanted to hole up at home. "Sorry."

I turned and left. Zach called out my name a couple of times, but I kept walking. My head hurt. My heart hurt. And I felt like a real idiot. This whole time, Benjamin knew I liked him. Had made fun of me behind my back.

Maybe I didn't know him like I thought I did.

When I got home, I kicked off my shoes and went right for the Oreos on top of the fridge. After four cookies, I managed to curb my depression hunger and dug my phone out of my pocket. I shot Josh a quick text asking him if he'd heard any rumors about me liking Benjamin.

Nothing, he replied. *I would have told you. :-P But lemme dig a bit.*

I sighed and ate another cookie.

"Camilla, is that you?" my mom called from the laundry room. "Did I hear the Oreos bag crinkle? You had better not be ruining your appetite for dinner."

"I'm eating my feelings, Mom," I yelled back. Then I snuck one more cookie, just because.

"I don't know what that means, but I am making a big stew for dinner, so I expect you to have your fair share."

My phone buzzed. A call from Joshua. Crud.

"Hey," I mumbled.

"Bad day?"

"You don't even know the half of it." I filled him in on my date fail, then my confrontation with Zach.

"Oh my God," he said when I finished. "That sounds awful."

"Yeah. I've already had, like, six Oreos."

"Okay, so my news doesn't get much better. I talked to a friend of Benjamin's who says yes, Benjamin did bring up that he'd caught you staring at him in class."

"Great." I banged my head on the kitchen table.

"Before you kill yourself, let me finish. Apparently, it was several months ago, well before you two started talking. And the friend didn't seem to think he was making fun of you. Just that he was recapping people in your class."

"So I became 'the starer,' then. Is that it?" My attempts at subtlety in checking him out had utterly failed. "Okay. Thanks for the update."

"If you want to hang out tonight, gimme a call."

We hung up. I dumped my book bag's contents all over the kitchen table and tried to drown myself in homework so I could forget what a crummy afternoon it had been. But when I saw the note Benjamin had passed me, the one I hadn't answered, tears welled in my eyes.

Time for more cookies.

CHAPTER SIXTEEN

Joshua

M adison," Tyler said as he cornered her outside the band room. "Come on. Talk to me. You can't keep ignoring me forever. This is killing me, babe."

I stood near the entrance and pretended to check my trumpet's keys. Yeah, I was nosy.

She sniffed and kept her attention on scanning the room. "I don't have anything to say to you."

"Seriously, this has gone on long enough. You're going to let one little thing like this break us up?" Tyler's eyes flashed with irritation. "I'm trying to be patient. I'm trying to talk to you. But you're freezing me out and for no good reason."

"It's *not* a little thing," she huffed. "Just because *you* don't see it as a good reason doesn't mean it isn't a good reason, because to me it *is* a good reason, and you're not, like, the good-reasons keeper, you know."

"I . . . What?" He blinked. The confusion was clear on his face. The guy was just totally not getting it. In all fairness, though, I'd barely followed her muddled point.

"Whatever." She waved her hand to push him away. "I don't have time for this bull. When you do figure it out, let me know." She marched into the band room, her flute case in hand.

"I'm trying to, Mad, but you won't help me," he called after her retreating figure. His gaze locked on mine, and I glanced away to pretend like I hadn't totally been eavesdropping. "Hey, Joshua." He stepped up to me. "What the hell am I supposed to do? You saw that—she isn't giving me a chance. She won't answer my phone calls. I can't even get her to talk to me in person."

I clapped a hand on his shoulder. "I think you're going about this the wrong way. You're making her feel bad for wanting a romantic gesture from you."

He stared at her, longing evident in his eyes. "I'd give her whatever she wanted. Why can't she just come out and tell me what I'm supposed to do?"

"Because that's not how it works. If she has to ask for it, then it doesn't feel sincere for her." I'd heard Camilla talk on and on about this very phenomenon, so I felt like an expert in understanding women. Okay, not really an expert—I doubted any guy could be. I shook his shoulder a bit so he'd look at me. "Madison wants to feel like you are going to sweep her off her feet, even if you guys have been together this long. In fact, the longer you're together, the harder you should work to keep making her feel special."

"Hmm. I guess I see your point. So I could do something big to win her back." He tilted his head in thought. "Maybe some kind of massive promposal in front of everyone in school."

What was it with guys and the overdoing-of-prom stuff? "No, no, no," I said. "Not big. Small. Simple. Romantic. *Sincere.* Don't make it about showing off how awesome you are. If you want to pluck at her heartstrings, you have to make her feel like she's the only woman for you. That you can't live without her."

His face turned serious, and he nodded. "I can't."

"Then make sure she knows that. Ask her to prom, Tyler. Do it like it's all on the line. Show her how much you love her. But until then, you have to leave her alone. Give her space so she feels what it's like to live without you. Let her have a chance to miss you. It'll make your reunion that much sweeter."

He gave me a nod of respect. "Thanks. You're pretty good at this, you know." He grinned.

"I spend a lot of time counseling my friends," I said with a snort.

Band went fast. Tyler fidgeted in his seat and seemed like he was going to jump up and run after Madison, but I gave him a stern look and shook my head. He got the message and instead waited until class emptied before leaving. Hopefully, the guy would figure things out. He was a little dense at times, but he meant well.

I grabbed my lunch bag and went to the cafeteria. Ethan was standing outside, arms crossed. As always, my heart lurched in my chest. He was supposed to have asked Noah to prom last Monday, but it hadn't happened for some reason. When I'd tried to subtly ask why, he'd told me it was the wrong day, that it hadn't felt right. The new date was going to be this Friday.

Which meant that Ethan was still single, and there was the tiniest bit of hope the promposal wouldn't happen.

"Hey, man," Ethan said as he gave me a friendly smile.

My pulse fluttered in my throat. "Hey, yourself." We walked

RHONDA HELMS

into the caf and sat at our usual table. Camilla was already there, eating a school burrito. "Forgot your lunch again, did you?" I asked her in a teasing tone.

She gave a miserable nod. "And this thing is heinous. It tastes like the lunch lady made it with her feet."

"Whereas my sandwich is delicious and nutritious, with no foot flavors in sight." I took a bite of my turkey sandwich, crafted to perfection with provolone, fresh lettuce, mayo, and mustard.

Her glare aimed at me could melt skin. "Rub it in, jerk."

"How are you?" Ethan asked her from over my shoulder.

We all knew what he meant. The crap with Benjamin and Zach.

She sighed and put down her fork. Her eyes looked tired, and I gave her a sympathetic smile. "Not too great. My prom date hates me, and the guy I like is pretending I'm not alive. Just another day in paradise."

I hugged her. "I'm sorry," I whispered. "I know how it feels."

"Know how what feels?" Ethan asked from behind me.

Caught up in my sadness for Camilla, I responded without thinking. "To want someone who doesn't want you back."

And instantly wished I could swallow my words.

Ethan's brows went almost into his hairline. "What? Who do you want?"

I scratched my neck as I tried to buy time to figure out a good answer. My impulsiveness was gonna get me into big trouble one of these days. I didn't know why I'd admitted it, and my heart was about to beat out of my chest. Maybe subconsciously I wanted him to sniff out the truth.

And when he finally did, it was going to ruin us.

"It's not that mall guy, is it?"

I blinked. "Who?"

Camilla elbowed me with a warning look, and my side flared with pain.

Oh. Crap. Right. The guy I'd made up. My fake possible prom date. I rubbed my ribs. "Um, no. It's not him. We're . . . not hanging out anymore." Yup, it was official—I was an idiot. I'd broken up with a guy who didn't even exist.

"So who is the guy, then?"

Man, he was unrelenting. I stiffened. "I don't really wanna talk about it right now." I cast an awkward glance at the other end of the table.

Not that they were paying any attention. Niecey and Dwayne were sucking face, and David was busy flirting with Ashley.

"Why not?" Ethan pressed.

My blood pressure spiked. Yeah, it was easy for Ethan to push and push and push for answers, because he didn't know the truth. "Because I said I didn't want to talk about it, okay?"

He stood and grabbed his stuff. His jaw was clenched so tightly I could envision his teeth cracking. "I'm always open with you. I don't think it's too much to expect the same in return." With that, he left.

My stomach flipped. "That went well."

"I'm sorry." Camilla rubbed my upper arm. "I didn't know what to say, so I just stayed quiet."

I thunked my head on the table. "How am I supposed to fix this? What can I say? If I go talk to him, he's going to want to know who I like. And I feel awful lying to him. Hell, I couldn't even pretend I liked someone who didn't exist."

"You're going to have to tell him sometime," she said.

"Yeah, because that worked out so nicely for you."

Her hand stopped, and I jerked my head up. Saw the flare of hurt and anger in her eyes.

"I'm sorry. That was uncalled for." Dammit. I was really digging myself in a hole here.

She gave me a stiff nod. "That's fine. I gotta go." She stood and picked up her lunch tray.

"Camilla, please." I poured everything I could into my eyes, into my voice. "I'm sorry. I wasn't trying to be a jerk. That came out wrong."

"I'll try to talk to Ethan," she finally said. "At least to get him off your back about who you like. But, Joshua, you can't keep this in forever. The longer you hide your secret, the more *that* will end up being the thing that wrecks your friendship. Not the confession itself."

"I know." I groaned and dropped my hands in my lap. "Thanks."

She leaned over, kissed my cheek, then left the cafeteria. And I tried not to stare in envy at the two happy couples sitting at the table. The people who had what I wanted the most.

Real love.

I strummed my guitar and played an old Elvis song I knew by heart. The chords were right, and the rhythm flowed perfectly. But my heart and soul weren't in it. I wasn't feeling it.

I stared at my bedroom walls and sighed as I put the guitar down on the bed. Milkshake jumped in my lap, and I gave her back a few absent strokes. Everything was wrong. I was . . . unsettled. Uneasy. Normally, I'd turn to Camilla and Ethan, but

Camilla was overwhelmed by her own problems, and Ethan *was* the problem.

Dad knocked on my door, then opened it and poked his head in. "I like that song you were playing."

Normally, I would have teased him about being old, but I didn't have the heart for it today. "Thanks."

Dad frowned and came in, sitting down beside me. "This isn't good for you, son. I don't like seeing you so unhappy. You're too young to be drowning in misery."

I sighed, bumped shoulders with him. "I'll get my act together soon, I promise. Did you finally finish writing your new book?"

He nodded and gave me a tired but satisfied smile. "Earlier today."

"I figured, since you emerged from the cave."

"Joshua, I'm gonna miss you when you go off to college. Who's gonna bust my chops about not showering or eating too much fast food?" His eyes turned sad for a moment, and he looked away.

My chest tightened. Everything was changing, and for one desperate moment I wished it could go back to the way it was before promposal madness set in, when Camilla and Ethan and I were close and happy. It would be easy to blame the changes in my world on Noah, but the truth was, Ethan was going to fall for someone eventually. I'd been biding my time, just waiting for it to happen.

"I promise to harass you from school," I said with a forced chuckle. "I'll make you send me pictures of your dinners to prove you're not living on cheeseburgers and frozen pizza."

He nodded and gave me a mock chuck under the chin. "Hang in there. You'll get through this."

"Thanks, Dad."

When he left, I stared at my guitar. The song I'd started for Ethan came to mind. I picked up the guitar and poured my emotions into finishing the song. He might never know the truth about its meaning, but at least I could get this off my chest for the moment. And avoid the massive thing that was lurking in the back of my head.

The fact that I'd made up my mind to tell Ethan on Friday how I felt about him.

CHAPTER SEVENTEEN

Camilla

I spent most of Thursday feeling lousy, a little under the weather. I wasn't sure if I'd caught a spring cold or what, but I had a headache and felt a little achy. Probably had nothing to do with all the drama in my life right now. Sure. I snorted as I popped by my locker on my way to statistics.

Before I entered class, a hand reached out and snagged my sleeve.

I spun around and saw Zach. Great. Just what I needed right now. He and I still hadn't talked since our big fight in the parking lot. I removed my arm from his grasp.

"Sorry," he said, a deep crease between his brows. "I . . . just wanted to get your attention without yelling."

A snotty comment popped into my head about how he hadn't bothered being subtle before, but I swallowed it. This wasn't the time to stoke the fires. "What's up?"

"I wanted to talk to you for a second." He cleared his throat. "I need to apologize for the way I behaved in our conversation. I was upset and acted badly."

Whoa. My jaw unclenched as I stared. I hadn't expected that. "Um, okay. Well, I'm sorry as well. I shouldn't have gone after you like that, when I was so mad." It was true; after taking time to mull it over, I realized I really should have calmed down before talking to him. My hotheadedness had started the whole thing.

"So, are we good? And do you still . . . want to go to prom with me? I promise not to hound you about it anymore. You do things on your own schedule. Just let me know what you need from me."

I gave a quick nod. "Yeah, that sounds good." No, things weren't fully settled yet between him and me, and I was still upset with the whole Benjamin situation, but it was a step in the right direction. The guy had a crush on me. I couldn't hate on him for that.

Zach and I went inside the classroom. I managed to make my way through statistics, then through the rest of my day until it was time for psychology. The class I used to love had become the class I dreaded most now.

I slid into my desk and kept my focus on my books, my notebook, the grain of my desktop, and the words carved into the corner. Carter was already present and asleep at his desk behind me.

Since Benjamin had turned me down, he and I hadn't communicated. Just awkward, painful silence. I was still mortified he'd talked about me, even if it had been before we'd been paired together. No one likes to feel like they are being laughed at, thought of as a creeper.

It was becoming easier not to think about Benjamin all the time. I certainly didn't allow myself to remember all our conversations, how we'd started getting closer. How we'd kissed.

That path led to madness. And I was done with deluding myself.

Yes, there was a possibility Benjamin had liked me. But not enough.

Stubborn pride kept me sitting in the seat behind him every day, despite my embarrassment. I didn't want him knowing that my feelings were hurt. I was going to pretend like I was totally fine. Like my heart wasn't crushed into tiny pieces.

Mrs. Brandwright was in rare form today. Calling on everyone in class, talking nonstop. She must have chugged coffee beforehand. Her upbeat nature pulled me out of my funk a bit, and I found myself responding.

Class went fast once I stopped moping around and focusing on how crappy I felt—both physically and emotionally. Truth be told, I was getting tired of being so down for days on end. It wasn't like me to stay this bummed this long. I'd never had a guy get to me like this.

I couldn't help it. I snuck a quick look at Benjamin. He was doodling on the sides of his notebook, body hunched over his desk. He rubbed the back of his neck, and I made myself not count the smattering of freckles.

Did he think about me at all?

My phone buzzed. I dug it out of my skirt pocket and peeked at the screen when Mrs. Brandwright had her back turned.

I'm doing it. Tmrw. Will try not to throw up on him.

Wow. I stared in shock at Joshua's message. *I'm proud of you,* I wrote back. *You got this. Lemme know if you need anything.*

I put my phone away before I could get busted—Mrs. Brandwright was pretty easygoing, but school policy was to take phones away when they were used in class. It was my lifeline. No way did I want it gone.

The last bell of the day rang. I quickly stood and gathered my

RHONDA HELMS

stuff, then ran out of class. When I got to my locker, I tucked my books in and reached for my stuff to go home.

"Camilla." The word was spoken so softly I almost didn't hear it over the noise in the hallway.

I sucked in a breath and spun on my heel, eyes locking with Benjamin. He peered down at me and chewed on his lower lip.

Was he . . . nervous?

"Hey," I replied. I leaned back against the edge of my open locker. My heart was doing the tango in my chest. I could smell him; I missed that scent.

Knock it off.

"How have you been?"

Polite conversation. Okay, I could do that too. "Fine, thank you. And you?"

"Not bad."

What do you want? I wanted to yell at him, because my stomach was all tied up in anticipation, anxiety. But I'd learned my lesson from the fight with Zach, so I kept my composure as best I could.

He sighed and leaned toward me, and I swear, for a moment his gaze flicked to my lips. "Have you read *Cyrano de Bergerac*?" he finally asked.

"Um, no?" What the hell? He wanted to resurrect that conversation method, right now, out of nowhere? I stared at him in confusion. "Should I?"

"I think you might find it illuminating." He crammed his hands in his back pockets and rocked on his heels. "Camilla. I'm . . . sorry." There was a low rumble as he said my name, and it edged its way through me. I wanted him to keep saying my name.

I wanted so many things.

"I've really enjoyed our talks," he continued. "And I didn't know how to reinstate them, given . . . you know, what happened."

"Yeah, I know." My cheeks flushed. "Sorry. I still feel like an idiot about that. Let's just pretend that didn't happen."

Benjamin took a step toward me, totally invading my space. This wasn't polite or friendly. This was assertive. He leaned down, and his lips just barely brushed the shell of my ear as he whispered, "Don't feel like that. You didn't do anything wrong. I just wish . . . I wish things were different."

My skin shivered from the contact. I tried so hard to fight my reaction, but I couldn't suppress it. I leaned closer to him, inhaled. God, why did he drive me so crazy? "Me too," I admitted.

He moved away, and I instantly missed his presence. Everything in my body was humming, aware of him. His eyes twinged with something that looked suspiciously like regret. "I gotta go."

I nodded, and he walked down the hall toward his locker. I couldn't help but stare at his retreating figure. Lean and strong and confident. No way had I imagined that moment between us.

I grabbed my stuff, closed my locker, and headed to the front doors. As I passed the girls' bathroom, I heard what sounded like a sob.

My feet stopped in place before I was even aware; then I moved to the bathroom door and gingerly opened it. "Hello?"

There was a heavy sniffle, but no one spoke.

I knew I should probably just leave the person alone. But instead, I walked in and closed the door behind me. The stall door at the end was open, and I slowly made my way toward it. "Hey, are you okay?"

Sitting on the toilet, fully clothed, was Karen. She dabbed at her eyes with a wad of toilet paper, and her red hair was a frazzled mess. When she glanced up and saw me, she stiffened. "Oh. Hey. I'm fine, thanks for asking. You can go."

The sight of makeup streaks down her cheeks made my heart melt. Despite her protests, she wasn't fine. I grabbed a paper towel, wet it, and handed it to her. "Toilet paper sucks for cleaning up crying messes on your face," I said. "Clumps and stuff, you know."

She eyed me but took the paper towel and wiped her cheeks with it. "Sorry. I've had a crappy day."

"I totally understand. I've been having a crappy couple of weeks."

Karen stood and made her way to the sinks. She splashed water on her face and dried it off with a fresh paper towel, then eyed herself in the mirror. Her sigh was long and heavy. "I'm ready for school to be over."

"Do you know where you're going in the fall?" I asked, trying to follow her conversation. I wasn't sure what was going on yet, but I decided to let her lead.

She nodded. "I got accepted to a school in Florida."

"That's great." I shifted from foot to foot. Should I leave? Maybe she wasn't going to open up, and I was just standing here like an idiot—

"Everything is going so wrong." Her words were quiet. She kept her gaze on her reflection, and I almost wasn't sure if she was talking to me or to herself. "I don't know how I messed it all up so badly. But I'm being stonewalled by every guy in school. No one will talk to me, much less ask me to prom."

Wow. My heart squeezed in a twinge of sympathy for her. After all, it could have been me just as easily as her. "Have you talked to David since he asked you?"

She stared at me through the mirror. "Why would I do that?"

I shrugged. "Maybe you'd feel better if you did. You were a little harsh in your answer to him."

Her nostrils flared.

I held up my hands. "Sorry, not trying to attack you. But it's possible guys are afraid you'd bust their balls like that too."

"I wouldn't do that, though." Her eyes flashed alarm.

"How do they know? They saw what happened with David," I pointed out.

She pursed her lips and clenched the water-spotted counter as she thought. "I didn't think I was that bad. But when I saw the video . . ." Her cringe was almost imperceptible. "I should have been gentler."

I took a step toward her and leaned my hip against the counter. "There's nothing wrong with going by yourself or with friends to prom. Don't let this ruin the end of your year." I paused and chewed over my next words. "And you'd probably feel better if you had a conversation with David about what happened. Maybe offered an apology."

It could also fix her relationship with Ashley. As far as I'd seen, the two girls hadn't hung out together since Ashley had asked David to prom.

"I'll think about it." With another small sniffle, she turned to me. "Thanks. I know we're not really friends . . . but I appreciate you listening."

"No problem." I offered her a small smile, then left the bathroom.

The hall was empty; I adjusted my backpack and left school. Funny enough, my joints weren't feeling that achy anymore. Maybe things were getting a little better.

CHAPTER EIGHTEEN

Joshua

I'm going to vomit."

"You're not going to vomit." Camilla wrapped her arm around my shoulder and moved me out of traffic toward the edge of the hallway. "It's going to be fine. I promise. Just try to relax."

My stomach was turning so hard I was sure it would leap out of my mouth. There was no way I was going to get through this without flipping my shit. I'd been a nervous wreck all day, unable to focus or function like, oh, regular human beings. Even my cat had hissed at me when I'd tried to pick her up this morning because my shaking hands had freaked her out.

And earlier, I'd flunked my English quiz because I'd been too busy thinking about what I was going to say to Ethan. Which had only made me even more distressed.

I stared down at my brown paper bag, filled with the bulk of my turkey sandwich and chips left over from lunch. I'd tried to take a bite of the sandwich earlier, but it had stuck in my stomach in a gross lump. Somehow, in my nervousness, I'd forgotten to toss the bag on my way out of the caf. "But what if I mess it all up and then he gets angry at me and—"

"Honey." She gripped the ice-cold fingers of my free hand and leaned her head toward me. Sympathy poured from her eyes into mine, and her confidence eased my tension a touch. "Whatever you say is going to come from the heart. You can't mess up how you feel—this isn't a mistake. The words will come, and they will be perfect."

Ethan had sent me and Camilla a text before lunch saying he was skipping. We both knew why—he was practicing his promposal.

And I was practicing my declaration of love.

"If anyone deserves happiness, it's you. I hope it all goes okay. But no matter what happens, I'm proud of you for this, you know." Camilla grabbed the lunch bag from me. She gave me a quick hug, and as she pulled back, I saw a hint of tears in her eyes. "Now go. Tell him how you feel. Break a leg."

"I think that's a theater saying."

She shrugged. "Then kick some ass. Whatever. You get the idea."

I gave her a tremulous smile as I walked down the hall toward the library, where Ethan was currently holed up. My pulse slammed in my ears. It was so hard to keep a cool smile on my face and wave and nod at people when I passed by. My limbs felt like they were being controlled by a puppeteer.

I made myself stroll. Drew in several long breaths and exhaled. I was in control. This was my choice, and I needed to do it. For the sake of our friendship and for the sake of my damn sanity.

And if he rejected me after I laid it all on the line, then . . . well, I'd deal with it at that time.

The library had a few students milling around, looking in the stacks for books. I wove through thick slabs of tables and made my way toward the back, where Ethan and I usually hung out whenever we studied in school. As expected, he was there, brown hair flopped over his brow, ankle crossing his thigh, foot twitching. In front of him was a sheet of paper he'd scrawled all over.

Nervousness practically oozed from his body.

"Hey," I said as I approached. I took a seat at the side of the table, leaving a few feet of space between us.

His eyes lightened a touch, though not as much as they normally did when we hung out. It was apparent he was distracted. "Hey, yourself. How was lunch?"

"Epic, as usual."

A dimple popped out when he smiled. "Really?"

"No, it was boring as hell. Literally nothing happened except a bunch of chewing." Well, not for me, since my stomach was too tense for me to eat, but whatever.

We both gave an awkward laugh. Wow. I didn't know who was more uncomfortable right now, me or him. It felt like all my muscles were knotted. Part of me wanted to jump up and run away.

I made myself ask, "So when are you asking him?"

"He's meeting me after school. I told him I needed to borrow some of his class notes." Ethan stared down at his fingers, which he was fiddling in his lap. He released them and pressed them to his thighs. "I'm going to mess this up."

An eerie echo of my earlier words to Camilla. I cleared my throat. "Um . . ." This was when I should be offering him advice or telling him it would go fine. In fact, there was still time. I could pretend I'd come here to support him, not to spill my guts.

But that was the coward's way, and I was tired of being a coward.

His brow furrowed, and for the first time since I'd arrived, he seemed to focus on me. "You okay, man?"

"Yes. No." Crap. I gave a small laugh. "Sorry."

He dropped his leg and leaned toward me. Those intense eyes pierced mine. Neither one of us spoke, and for one crazy second I was so, so tempted to grab the back of his head and slam his lips against mine.

Would he freak?

Or would he kiss me?

I tried to shake off that mental image and regroup. Do or die time. "I need to talk to you, Ethan. If you have a minute."

He seemed to sense my seriousness, because he didn't move, just stared hard at me. "Okay."

"Do you remember back in seventh grade, when we realized both of us were gay?"

He blinked in obvious confusion over what seemed like a random statement. "Yeah. Why?"

I could recall that day so well. It was early fall, and Ethan and I had been standing on the sidelines outside in gym class, waiting for our turn to kick the ball. The tall kid who went before us was the most attractive guy in our whole school, with blue eyes that had long lashes.

Up until that point in our friendship, Ethan and I hadn't discussed homosexuality. Wasn't exactly something young teens got into while working on homework or whatever. Nor had I really had much suspicion that Ethan was gay, too. Until I saw the way he had looked at that guy in gym class. Like he was attracted to him.

A fleeting glimpse, but enough to make me realize I wasn't alone in how I felt about boys.

That day, after school, I'd confessed to Ethan I was gay. He'd told me the same. Of course, a couple of weeks later, we'd both realized the hot blue-eyed guy was a huge douchebag and lost our attraction to him. But our friendship stayed cemented.

"You and I made a pact that day not to hide anything big from each other," I said.

He raised an eyebrow. "What, are you going to tell me you like girls now?"

I tried to smile at his attempt to lighten the mood. "Um, no." My palms grew damp, and I rubbed them on my thighs. My heart jackhammered in my chest. "Ethan, I'm in love with you."

My words were almost whispered, but he heard them. He stilled.

A flush crawled up my throat and across my cheeks, and I dropped my attention to my brown loafers. "I've loved you since the first day I met you. I love the way you light up when you hear a song you like. I love how you stick your tongue out when you're deep in thought and studying. I love how you support my music."

"Joshua." His voice was choked; I didn't dare look up.

I couldn't seem to stop talking. "I know you have a crush on Noah. And I know he's everything I'm not—he's sexy and confident and multitalented and exotic. But I've been in love with you for years, and for the sake of our friendship, I needed to tell you."

Silence.

We sat that way for a good minute. I hadn't realized how long a minute could last until I was holding my heart in my hands. Waiting to hear what the guy I loved would say in response to my declaration.

RHONDA HELMS

I finally looked up at him. Saw . . . a touch of anger in his eyes. Confusion. And a healthy dollop of fear.

"I can't believe you're doing this right now," he told me in a low tone I couldn't interpret.

The air locked in my chest.

Ethan ran a hand through his hair. "I . . . don't know what to say. What to think."

I leaned back in my chair and scratched the stubble on my jaw. Struggled to draw my breath. "I realize this is coming out of nowhere for you. But you have to understand, this has been eating away at me for so long . . . partly because I was petrified it would ruin our friendship. Yeah, I knew this might wreck it, but I had to say it anyway."

Something flared in his eyes, a light of recognition. "So the guy you said you have a crush on . . ."

"Yeah," I confirmed with a small, bitter laugh. "It was you. But how could I possibly tell you that when you kept asking me? After all, we're just friends, right?"

He didn't answer me. His gaze skittered away from mine, and in that gut-sinking moment I realized I'd lost him. His heart wasn't with me—I'd been an idiot to think I had a chance. Not when Noah was around.

I stood and tried to gather the tattered scraps of my pride. "Anyway, I had to tell you. Because we're friends. Best friends. And if I couldn't be true and honest with my best friend without my honesty destroying us, then we didn't have a real friendship to begin with."

Ethan still wouldn't meet my eye. His jaw tensed. "This blind-sided me, Joshua. I . . . I need some time."

I clenched my hands into tight fists so he wouldn't see them wobble. All I could manage was a nod; my lungs were painfully squeezed right now.

I turned and walked away.

Left Ethan, the guy I loved beyond anything else, behind.

And he didn't say a word, just let me go.

Each step hurt more than the last. The fear that I'd lost him for good wouldn't stop taunting my mind. What was I supposed to do now? Had I messed everything up by being honest?

Maybe it wasn't solely the confession that had screwed things up. Maybe it also had been the wrong time to tell him—I probably should have done this a few days ago. In my need to purge myself of my feelings, I hadn't thought about the impact it would have on him.

Ethan had already had his mind set on asking Noah, and I'd walked in and thrown a big twist into his plans. Had added a new layer of stress to what was already a stressful day. *Nice going, Mendez,* I told myself.

The bell for class rang. Students spilled into the hallway. I slipped through the chaos, my body moving forward of its own volition like a zombie. My emotions had completely shut down, and for the moment I felt nothing but blissful numbness.

I'd finally told him. No matter what happened from here on out, I'd conquered my biggest fear.

But now I felt lost, without direction. So I walked to the empty, dark band room and sat in a chair. Stared blindly at the scattered music stands, chairs, percussion instruments. No, I hadn't expected Ethan to jump into my arms and tell me he secretly loved me too. But was it wrong that a small part of my heart had hoped for it?

Nor had I expected such anger, such frustration from him.

Shock, yes. But not that strong outpouring of negativity. Or fear. So much for priding ourselves on our honest friendship. It must have been all in my head.

Okay, that wasn't true. I knew that. But my bitter heart was aching and overreacting.

Camilla would want to know how it went, but I refrained from sending her a text. I just wanted to silently sit and figure out what I was going to do. How I was going to pick myself up and get through the rest of today.

CHAPTER NINETEEN

Camilla

I hate statistics," I declared as I tossed my pen across our kitchen table. My head throbbed, so I rubbed the tender spots at my temples. "It's stupid. Who cares about how many slices of pizza a female employee eats versus a male employee? Why can't we get more interesting problems to work on?"

Josh rolled his eyes. "Because it's high school, and high school is dull. This isn't new information. And no, you don't hate statistics. You're actually good at it, Miss A-plus in math every year."

"Ugh. I know." I gave a heavy sigh and propped my head on my chin. "I just wanted to wallow in a little self-indulgent whininess for a while."

That got him to laugh, which eased the stress in the kitchen a bit. Right now it was thick enough to cut with a knife and serve on a platter. Between me missing Benjamin and Joshua fretting over Ethan, we were hot messes all around.

Joshua thunked his head on the table. "Camilla, I feel like an idiot. It's been five days and he still won't talk to me." He lifted his head, and when his gaze fixed on mine, I could see the dark smudges under his eyes. "Have you heard anything from him lately?"

I rubbed his back. "No, but these things take time." When I'd gone up to Ethan on Monday to say hi and see how he was, he'd given me a shaky smile and a quick hug. I could tell Joshua's confession had really shocked him, and I'd been too afraid to ask him how the promposal went with Noah. Other than that, I hadn't seen Ethan much at all. "Keep in mind, you've known your feelings for years. He's known them for a few days. It's a big thing for him to sort through."

"I know. I just . . . I thought I'd have heard something by now. I left him alone all weekend except that one text I sent him on Sunday, saying I'd be happy to talk whenever he was ready. His reply was a curt 'Okay.'"

It killed me to see Joshua suffering so much. He wasn't one to walk around bummed out and full of self-pity. I could tell he was trying to keep his chin up, to act like this wasn't tearing him apart. But the shadows in his eyes were too big to overlook.

"Ethan has to do this at his own pace." Boy, it was easy for me to dole out romance advice when it didn't relate to my own ridiculous love life. Or lack thereof. "Anyway, you tried. I tried. We gambled on love, and it appears like we lost. But at least we played the game, and that's what's important."

Joshua snorted, and I saw my hokey words had a rousing effect on him. He shook his head. "You should write a self-help book."

"Maybe I will." I jutted my chin in the air. "*How to Look Super Awkward and Blow Your Chances with the Guy You Like.* I smell a hit."

We worked in silence for the next few minutes, pausing only to ask each other questions about random homework things.

"I'm going to miss this, you know," I told him. My throat tightened with unexpected emotion.

He looked up at me, a brow raised. "What do you mean? You'll miss all this glorious homework?" He waved a hand over the table.

"No. I'm going to miss being able to see you every day when we graduate and move away." I sighed. Everything was going to change. I wouldn't be able to sneak in Joshua's bedroom window at night to hang out and talk, or have impulsive Sunday-afternoon shopping trips. "Maybe it's not too late for me to join you in New York City. There's nothing holding me to this place anyway."

"I'll just sneak you into my dorm room. No one will ever know."

"I'll get a side job dancing on a street corner."

He nodded his approval, a crooked smirk on his face. "Now you're thinking. That's the surefire route to success."

If only that would really work. But I'd already accepted at the local college, deciding it was the most economical choice. Another lovely four years of living at home. *Whee.* That thought made me slump.

"Chin up," he said, and I saw the sadness in his eyes, which strangely made me feel better—I wasn't alone in this. "I'll come visit you every chance I can. And have you visit me too."

I nodded and tried to shake off my blues. Yeah, it would be different. But we were too good of friends for distance to come between us. I had to have faith.

Mom came into the kitchen and eyed the two of us. "Are you two working or are you spending all afternoon yapping?"

Ah, good old Mom. Some things would never change. For once I appreciated her constant nature. "We're getting work done."

"And yapping," Joshua said under his breath.

Mom shot him the evil eye; apparently, she'd heard him. But a moment later, a thoughtful expression crossed her face, and she spun on her heel and headed to the kitchen counter. Tucked away was a foil-wrapped pan.

"What's that?" I asked.

She ignored me, peeled the foil off, and then grabbed plates. When she came back over to the table, I saw she'd brought us two huge slices of chocolate cake with chocolate frosting. My favorite. He and I both perked up.

"You two look far too doom and gloom," she declared. "And skinny. Mama's cake will fatten your cheeks and make you feel better."

I gave her a small hug. "Thanks, Mom."

"I'm going to miss your cake," Joshua said in all seriousness. I agreed—yeah, my mom was a nutbar, but her cake was out of this world.

She took an empty seat opposite us and plopped her arms on the table. "Okay. What is wrong with you guys? It is like a stranger kicked your dog or something. I have never seen such frowning faces."

I dug into my cake with gusto. I knew exactly what she was doing—bribing us with sugary goodness to get us to talk to her. Unfortunately, her mad scheme was working. "It's been a crappy few weeks," I told her as I tried to select the right words. "I like a guy, but he doesn't like me." Or not enough, anyway. But the situation was far too complicated to try to explain to her. "And Joshua's having some love issues as well."

Mom nodded. She reached over and scooped a bite of my cake. "Ah, so you finally told Ethan, did you?" she asked him.

He blinked and sat in stunned silence for a moment. "Wait, you knew too? How is it everyone knew but Ethan?"

"Please." Mom waved my fork as she rolled her eyes. "It was so obvious. What, do you think parents are blind or something? We do know what love is. After all, we made you children."

Joshua barked a laugh.

I groaned. "Mom, God, stop. I don't want to talk about you and Dad having . . ." I couldn't make myself finish the sentence.

She huffed. "Well, it's true."

My phone buzzed on the table. I glanced at the display. *RU free to quickly meet and go over prom details this wk? NOT nagging you. Just checking.*

The phone buzzed again with an additional message from Zach. *Prom is just 2½ weeks away . . .*

Crap. He was right. How had time flown away from me this fast? I swallowed, then forced a wide, easy smile to my face before anyone could ask me questions.

"Who was that texting you?" my mom asked, because God forbid she not know everything going on in this house. Her eyes narrowed at me and she thinned her lips. "Was it that boy who is your prom date? Zach? What's happening with that, and why haven't we seen him around lately? You *are* still going with him, right?"

Wonderful. I shrugged, even as guilt ate away at my stomach. "Yeah, it was him, but it wasn't a big deal. I'll deal with it ASAP, I promise, Mom." Well, as soon as I could muster some excitement for prom, I would. Not even the allure of dressing up for a night could make me excited about this. I'd been dragging my feet for weeks now, and it was finally starting to bite me in the ass.

"Not a big deal?" She squinted. "Young lady, you haven't even gotten your dress yet. How is that not a big deal? Are you brushing this boy off?"

"Whoa, really?" Joshua asked me, wide-eyed. "You haven't bought anything for prom? Why not?"

My face burned, and I crossed my arms. "Guys, I really don't want to deal with the inquisition right now, if you don't mind. I do have homework to finish." I waved at the papers.

"Camilla." Mom's eyes softened, and she reached over and patted my hand. "I know you don't have feelings for him, but he has feelings for you. You must give this boy a chance. It is only right. We will go tonight and purchase you a dress. No arguments," she said to cut off my next words. She rose from the table. "It won't be as lovely as your aunt would have made you, but we have run out of time. Finish your homework like a good girl, and eat the rest of your cake." Her hand gently patted my cheek, and she left.

"Your mom is right, you know," Josh said.

"That I'm a good girl?" I snorted. "Hardly."

"Hon, you did tell him you would go with him to prom. Why haven't you gotten your dress and accessories yet? What's making you drag your feet so much? This isn't like you."

I bit my lower lip. "I just don't feel excited about it. With you down in the dumps over Ethan and possibly not even going to prom and me being forced to go with someone who's barely a friend, it isn't something I'm stoked to do. I mean, what's the point? It's going to be awkward, and all I'm going to do is think about Benjamin. Which I know is totally unfair to Zach, but it's true." I sighed and dropped my head in my hand. "Why can't I let him go and stop thinking about him so much? He doesn't want me, but I can't get him out of my head."

He reached over and took my hand. Squeezed it. "I know how you feel. Trust me."

"I wish you and I could go together, instead. We'd have so much fun." I pleaded with him with my eyes. "Is there any way I can get you to consider coming to prom? I'll help pay for your tux, even. And I'm pretty sure there's still time to buy a ticket, or we can beg for one somehow."

He glanced away, and I saw a flash of pain before he donned a small smile.

"I'm sorry," I said quickly. "It was selfish of me to ask." I wouldn't want it rubbed in my face either. How could I blame him for being so hesitant?

"No, don't be sorry. Friends are supposed to be there for each other." He gave a heavy, painful sigh. "Besides, I bought a ticket last week, just in case."

My eyes filled with tears and my throat tightened. I reached over and hugged him. "Really? So you'll go?"

He hugged me back. "Like I'd miss the opportunity to see you dolled up. You're going to look fabulous."

"You will too. I can't imagine any guy in there who will rock a tux harder than you will."

He laughed. "Girl, please. We both know that's the truth."

"As long as you save all the good dances for me." I'd do my best to make sure Joshua had a great time at prom. That he wouldn't be hurting badly over Ethan.

Suddenly I felt renewed, even a touch excited at the thought of dress shopping. No, it wasn't what I'd wanted to happen. But

I'd have a great night with my best friend. I would stop holding Zach at arm's length and actually make an effort to friend him. Not this half-assed wading-through-life thing I'd been doing the last few weeks.

I was done with being down. Joshua needed me, and I was determined to be there for him.

We finished our homework, and he headed home. I put my homework away in my room and stretched out on my bed, arms crossed behind my head. I probably wasn't going to stop having these feelings for Benjamin for a long time. But that was okay—or it would be, anyway. He'd impacted my life in ways he didn't know. I found myself thinking deeper, examining music and books in a way I never had before.

Hmm. That reminded me—hadn't he suggested a book to me the last time we'd talked, at my locker? Shit, what was it he'd said, and why hadn't I written it down?

I scrambled to think. Ah, that was the day I'd found Karen in the bathroom, crying over no one asking her to prom. I'd gotten distracted.

Cyrano de something or other. Yeah, that was it. All I knew about Cyrano was my mom watching some eighties movie based on the book, where the romantic lead had a huge nose or something.

I jumped up and rushed to my computer. Oh, wow. Apparently the whole thing was available online. I opened it and began to read, starting with the summary.

The air locked in my lungs, and I stared dumbly at my screen. *No way.* There was no way Benjamin would be giving me a message like this. Would he? That was crazy. I read the summary again. The two men in the play were close. Both had feelings for the same woman. And Cyrano had to push aside his feelings so his friend could woo her and win her hand.

What had he said specifically to me? That I'd find it "illuminating."

My stomach began a wild flutter, like a thousand butterflies were trying to burst free. Oh my God. If this was true . . .

Maybe Benjamin liked me a lot after all.

CHAPTER TWENTY

Joshua

I picked at my school salad with my fork. The lettuce was veering on limp, and the oily dressing gave the greens a greasy look. I shot an exaggerated frown at Camilla. "How do you eat this stuff all the time?"

"You're just picky." She dug into her salad with gusto. "It's not that bad if you eat it fast."

"Yeah, that sounds like a winning plan. I must be the only one in our whole school who doesn't find this satisfying." I snorted.

Ignoring me, she finished chewing her bite, then put her fork down. Dabbed the corners of her mouth with her napkin. Then she drew in a deep breath and spun in her chair to face me. "Can I talk to you about something that seems *really* crazy at first but actually might not be?"

"Sounds right up my alley." I grinned.

Her eyes grew serious as she leaned toward me. "So . . . I think Benjamin gave me a secret message that he likes me. But I'm not sure if I'm reading into it or not. I was up for hours last night thinking about it, and it's driving me batty, and I need another person's perspective."

Wow. "A secret message? That sounds fun. What did it say?"

"Well . . . " She chewed on her lip and glanced away. "Okay, it wasn't like a text or note or anything. It was a book."

"He gave you a book?"

"No, no." She waved a hand. "Let me explain."

Over the next couple of minutes, Camilla summed up the notes she and Benjamin had passed back and forth in class, discussing books and music and stuff. How they'd been giving each other recommendations and analyzing them. Of course, this had happened before she'd asked him out.

"So last week, out of the blue, he told me I should read *Cyrano de Bergerac*, but I forgot all about it. He hasn't mentioned anything to me since, and I can't figure out why. Either A, I didn't read it quickly enough and he's too embarrassed to bring it up now, or B, I'm reading more into the book's meaning than he meant and it wasn't that big of a deal." She pursed her lips and turned pleading eyes to me. "And the thing is, I really can't tell which it might be. Because he was pretty firm in telling me to read the book. So it has to mean something, right? I'm not just being weird here?"

I dug through my memory bank. "Hmm. That's the one where the ugly guy likes the hot girl, and his hot friend likes her too, right?"

She nodded.

"But . . . didn't the girl also like the hot guy or something?"

"Yeah. Both guys liked the girl, but at first she only liked the handsome one, not Cyrano. It's not a perfect fit for our situation, but I don't know if that matters here. I *for sure* do not like Zach like that, and Benjamin knows it." She sighed. "But I'm too afraid to ask him what he actually meant."

"Because if it wasn't a message about him having feelings for you, it will hurt to find that out." I gave her a sympathetic smile.

"And I'll be even more mortified than I already am." She bit her thumbnail. "So I'm stuck—what do I do? Should I mention I read the play and see what he says? Or has it been too long now?"

I rubbed my jaw. "I know it's tempting to read into it—and trust me, I don't blame you. I'd be doing the exact same thing. But the guy hasn't said anything to you since then, right?"

She shook her head, her face miserable. "But I don't know if that's because I hadn't read it yet and he's waiting for me to. Maybe this was him putting the ball in my court."

"Yeah. Maybe."

"You don't sound sure."

"I guess I feel like if he's going to tell you something, wouldn't he be more obvious and open about it? That seems too subtle. Would he make you work this hard to figure out he likes you? After all, since all this began, he hasn't given you any signs that he's into you. This just seems too random."

She sucked in a loud breath. "Well . . ."

I raised an eyebrow. "Whoa. Are you holding back on me?"

"We . . ." She leaned closer and whispered in my ear, "We did kiss. A while ago, while working on our psych project at the mall."

"Why didn't you tell me?" Part of me was hurt by her silence.

"Because it didn't happen again. And I felt dumb. And . . ." She flushed, her cheeks staining a pretty pink. "I just—I wanted to savor it. If that makes sense."

I nodded. I got it. If the guy I loved kissed me, it would be too special to blab about to everyone. Still . . . "I'm your best friend. You know I wouldn't have gossiped about it to anyone." The irony of the situation struck me, and my guilt flared. Ethan had been upset at me for keeping secrets too.

"I know. I'm sorry." She gave me a chagrined smile. "After a while, it seemed like it was a nonevent, since nothing happened. So I tried to forget it happened. Until he told me to read that book. Which is why I'm torn."

I sipped my Dr Pepper. "Yeah, that does change things a bit." I rested my hands on my thighs. "But I don't know. I feel like he could be much more open if he was telling you he liked you. Even with his cousin liking you too. That seems awfully subtle."

"Yeah. I guess you're right." She poked at her salad, eyes down-turned, back hunched over.

I hated making her sad. But I also didn't want to fill her with false hope if he was just going to hurt her feelings again. "I'm sorry. Maybe I'm wrong." I nudged her with my side to get her to look at me and offered a small smile. "Wouldn't be the first time."

"Hey, guys." Ethan plopped down in the seat beside me and opened his lunch bag. "Sorry I'm late. I had to talk to my German teacher."

I blinked and stared at him, my jaw practically hitting the ground. Even Camilla was quiet as we both sat there, shocked.

Ethan's eyebrows shot up. "What? Am I not allowed to sit here anymore?"

"Um, no, by all means." I waved at the seat.

He gave me a brief nod, then bit into his sandwich. I ripped my gaze away and fixed my attention back on my pathetic salad. It was hard, forcing myself to eat, but that was better than letting myself

RHONDA HELMS

think about how very, very close he was to me. I could feel the heat of his body pouring into my side. His thigh even brushed mine for a fraction of a second as he shifted in his seat. And that familiar scent of his skin and bodywash wafted toward me.

Don't you dare close your eyes and breathe him in, I ordered myself. In punishment for my weakness, I ate a huge bite of crappy salad.

Ethan made small talk with David and Ashley, whose hands were pretty much cemented together now. Since their promposal, I hadn't seen them apart. Funny how that crush he'd had on Karen had faded when he was faced with real, sweet, true affection. Ashley was good for him, and it made me glad to see them working out.

It also made me painfully aware of how much I missed my easy relationship with Ethan. Those extended days of silence after my confession had stung me immeasurably. For the hundred thousandth time, I wished I hadn't told him how I felt.

Well, that wasn't quite true. I wished he'd reacted differently.

But he was here now, and maybe that meant he was ready to pretend like it never happened, for us to go back to being friends. Could we? Was that what I wanted?

Yes.

And no.

It was so hard not to confront him and ask him what was going on with us. And with Noah. How had the promposal gone—had Noah said yes? I'd be damned if I asked Ethan about it, though. And somehow I doubted he'd offer up details anyway.

"—don't you think, Joshua?" Ethan was saying.

I stiffened, caught off guard. I hadn't paid attention to the conversation. "Uh . . ."

David rolled his eyes and grinned. "We're talking about how fast the school year is flying now that it's almost over."

"Yeah. It sure is." My heart gave a dull ache, and I stood. I needed a moment to gather myself before I could sit here and fake like everything was okay. Just a minute to tuck my raw feelings deep down in my chest. "I'm gonna get a piece of cake. I'll be back in a sec."

I didn't want cake. But it was a handy excuse to escape. I walked through the line and grabbed a plate of carrot cake. To help shake off my inner tension, I listened to the casual conversations around me. I moved as slowly as I could to the cashier.

It worked. As I headed back to the table, my happy mask was back in place. I sat down and dug into my cake, even though I didn't taste a thing. Smiled and laughed at jokes. Camilla shot me a concerned glance, but I kept up the facade and served her a cheeky wink. She wasn't fooled, but she didn't call me out on it.

Ethan, however, was totally fooled. For once. Go figure.

The bell ending lunch rang. It was incredibly hard to stand and walk away from the table like I didn't have a care in the world. All I wanted to do was grab Ethan by the shoulders and ask him why he didn't love me.

After I dumped my trash, I turned and almost ran face-first into Ethan. He laughed and held his hands up to keep me from falling over. "Whoa, you okay?" he asked.

My smile was brittle; the facade was cracking. "I'm fine, thanks."

I saw a flare in his eyes, but it was gone before I could label the emotion. He gave me a polite smile. "Okay. I'll see you later."

He strolled out the door, and I had to fight to keep from running after him. I just couldn't do it. I'd laid everything on the line in the library. Had bared my heart to him, told him I loved him. If he wanted to talk, it was up to him.

Camilla came up and threaded her arm through mine. "You okay?"

We left the caf. "I will be," I answered her. Ethan's figure was absorbed into the crowd, and he disappeared. I sighed. "That was so hard."

"I know." She rested her head on my upper arm for a moment. "My first impulse was to yell at you to go talk to him. But I already knew what you'd say to that."

I kissed her forehead and gave her a gentle smile. "It's out of my hands. If Ethan wants to pretend things are normal, I'll just have to pretend right along with him until they are." And someday it wouldn't hurt as much as it did right now.

We went our separate ways. I stopped by my locker to grab my books for class. I shuffled down the hallway, and in the entryway of a classroom I saw Tyler clutching Madison's hands. Her face had hesitation written all over it.

I slipped closer.

"—messed up, Mad. I realize that now," Tyler was saying. He sucked in a ragged breath. I could see the intensity in his eyes as he stared at Madison. Like she was everything to him. I'd never seen him that serious before.

She swallowed, and her hands began to shake. Her back was stiff, but her eyes were locked on him. "You really hurt me."

"I did. And it was wrong. I made you feel like you were unimportant. Like you weren't worth my best effort. It's taken me a while to understand it, but I do now." He dropped down to one knee and dug into his pocket. With flourish, Tyler revealed a ridiculously huge Ring Pop with a shiny red candy stone on top.

Madison chuckled, even as her eyes grew damp. A curious crowd joined me around the doorway, and a few girls sighed audibly.

"I've never known anyone as sweet as you." He kissed the ring finger of her left hand, then slid the candy ring on. When he turned his gaze back to her eyes, there was a warmth in there that hit me square in the gut. No one had ever looked at me like that before—like I was the center of his world. "You make me the happiest guy in school, Madison. I know it's *really* late to ask, and I'm an idiot. And if you say no, I will understand. But I'd be honored if you would attend prom with me. I am so in love with you, and I will continue to be, even if we aren't together anymore. I miss you so much, babe."

"Do it," a girl beside me whispered.

Madison swallowed and licked her lips. With a trembling breath, she said to Tyler, "You're super lucky I bought my dress back in September."

Hope lit his face, and he stood. His face was tight with anticipation. "So is that . . . ?"

"Yes." She beamed at him and wrapped her arms around his neck. "Yes, I will go to prom with you, you goofball." Madison pressed a warm kiss on him, and he wrapped her in his arms.

The growing crowd exploded with whistles and claps. I joined in. *Good for you, Tyler,* I cheered silently. Madison wouldn't have to worry again about feeling taken for granted. He'd learned from the experience and had proven that to her with that simple but heartfelt promposal. Kinda made me feel like I had a part in them reuniting.

I let that happy thought buoy me out of my own inner darkness as I wandered to my next class.

CHAPTER TWENTY-ONE

Camilla

Tuesday of prom week. I could hardly believe it was almost time—not to mention that school was about to end. Yesterday I'd been such a flake in my classes, despite upcoming finals. But the end was near, and I could make it.

It didn't help that I'd been torn for days about what to do regarding Benjamin. Over the last week or so, I'd started writing to him a dozen notes suggesting we talk about the book, but I'd tossed them all away. Everything made me sound like a dork, like I was trying too hard.

But yesterday I'd caught him looking at me as I walked into the room before class. He'd ripped his hot gaze away from mine before I approached our row, but I knew what I'd seen. A hint of interest in his eyes. Something deep and resonant, like the looks we'd exchanged before I'd asked him out.

I was going to talk to Benjamin today about the book, once and for all. I needed answers, whether I'd like them or not.

Statistics class was so hard to focus in. It didn't help that from across the room, I could feel Zach's quiet gaze on me. Despite his intense stares in every class, he hadn't talked to me for quite a while now, other than the rare occasional text. Apparently, he was going to keep his promise and quit hounding me. My mom's words from before rang in my head about how I needed to give him a chance.

I knew she was right, and remorse had twisted my stomach over the last few days as I'd considered her advice. I should talk to him today after class, if only to ease this lingering tension between us. He had respected my boundaries; I should show him I appreciated the effort.

When the bell was over, I darted outside and waited for Zach. Soon he appeared through the door. When I stepped in front of him, he stopped and jerked a bit.

"Oh, hey. Is . . . everything okay?"

I nodded. "Do you have a sec?"

"Sure, sure." We moved away from the crowd. His body was stiff as he stood and stared at me. He crossed his arms over his chest and waited in silence.

My heart gave an irregular beat. "Um. I just wanted to say . . . well, a lot of things. First, thank you for not pushing me so hard about prom anymore."

"You're welcome," he quietly replied. "You know, I've done a lot of thinking. I was a jerk to you." I went to open my mouth, but he held up a hand. "Wait. Let me finish. This is hard enough for me to say. I liked you—*like* you. From the first time I met you, I thought you were smart and funny. You make class fun with your smile and laughter."

My heart squeezed. "That's so sweet of you. Thank you."

He shrugged. "Of course I wanted to go to prom with you. Who wouldn't? You're perfect."

God, no. I shook my head and laughed. "Oh man, I'm so not perfect. I screw up everything."

"I don't mean you're flawless." He paused, scrunched up his face as he struggled to explain. "I mean . . . well, I think you're everything a guy could ever want in a girl. It's taken me a while to remove my head from my ass, but I know you don't like me like that. And that's okay."

I sighed. "I'm sorry."

"No, really. It's okay. I know you like Benjamin, and I was unfairly rude to you about that. I wanted to hurt you and I exaggerated the truth. He doesn't go around talking about you like that—if anything, I've only ever heard him say nice things."

I admit, my heart skipped a beat at that.

"I know we're really late in the year and prom is just around the corner." He drew in a deep breath and seemed to steel himself. "But if you want to break off prom with me and go with someone else, I'll let you go with no hard feelings. I promise."

Everything stilled around me for one long, tempting moment. I could walk away from him without it blowing up in my face. Maybe take a chance and see if Benjamin would want to come with me, despite it being just a few days away.

Then I looked into Zach's eyes and saw the angst, the emotion. I couldn't do that to him. No, I didn't have feelings for him, but we could be friends. And friends didn't treat each other like that.

I stepped closer and squeezed his arm. "That's really nice of you. I appreciate it because I know you mean it. But I'm totally good with being your prom date. As friends, of course," I added. Just so we were both clear.

The tension leaked from his body at my words, and he smiled. Nodded. "Yes. Friends. Okay."

"Besides, I already bought my dress, and this particular shade of red won't match anyone else there," I teased. Mom had dragged me from store to store until I'd found one I loved, along with a matching pair of heels. It was unfortunate Benjamin would never see me in my foxiest outfit ever, but I'd dance my feet off anyway and have a good time with my friends.

His grin was almost wide enough to split his face in two. "Okay. I'll see you later, then."

We went our separate ways. My next class, English, was meeting in the library for study time, so I ran all the way there to avoid being late. I made it just before the bell rang, dumped my bag on a nearby table, and headed to the stacks. My teacher saw me and gave me a nod of acknowledgment.

I wandered down the aisle to find a good resource for my final paper. But I had a hard time focusing. My chest felt lighter somehow; resolving that stuff with Zach had been more freeing than I'd realized it would be.

I shot Joshua a brief text. *I talked to Zach and we worked things out. Feeling much better.*

My phone buzzed. *Good. I know that's been stressful. Hugs. BTW meet me outside *right* after bell.*

Okay . . . ? Why? I wrote back.

He replied with a picture obviously taken from his lap, his face stern. *No arguments. We're hanging out today.*

Yes, sir. I chuckled quietly as I fired back my reply, then returned my attention to the library books. When I found one that seemed to fit, filled with autobiographical information, I plucked it off the shelf and headed to my table.

The next half hour passed fast. I focused on work, took notes, made good headway on my paper. I was proud of myself for buckling down and focusing. My hand flew across the notebook as I wrote my thoughts.

Someone sat down at the table across from me and cleared his throat. I looked up and nearly dropped my pencil in surprise.

"Benjamin. You're not in my English class." Duh. Could I sound any dumber? Of course he wasn't, and we both knew it. I bit back an embarrassed sigh.

"You catch on fast." His mouth curved into a ghost of a smile. I drank in the unexpected pleasure of seeing him. He had on a slim-fitting white T-shirt, and his dark blond hair was in messy spikes on his head. "I'm studying for an upcoming test."

This was my chance. If only my stomach would stop trying to burst its way out of my abdomen. I dropped my hands in my lap to hide their nervous shake. "So. I . . . I read *Cyrano de Bergerac.*"

Surprise flew across his face, but he covered it quickly. "I figured you might have forgotten about it, since I didn't hear anything."

He was good at this. I couldn't read into his words at all. So I chose mine carefully. "I hadn't read it before, but I did find it interesting. Really interesting. In fact, I sat up most of the night reading it. My heart broke for poor Cyrano."

His eyes grew heavy-lidded, and he nodded. "It's a tough spot to be in."

"Have you ever been in a spot like that?" And, oh God, that

was about as forward as I could make myself get. Even that much of a confrontation made my pulse throb under my skin.

His nod was so faint I could barely see it. Our eyes were locked dead on each other, and neither of us looked away.

The bell rang, and I immediately wanted to smash the stupid thing into pieces. No! We were just starting to get somewhere.

He gave a short laugh and shook his head. "I guess we'll have to save the rest of this conversation for another time."

"Maybe during psych?"

"We have a quiz, remember?"

Oh crap. No, I'd completely forgotten. Wonderful. I hadn't even studied for it.

I gathered my things, and we walked to the library doors. I wanted this moment to stretch on forever. "When are you free?"

"So you are still interested in . . . the book?" There was a strange uncertainty in his voice that surprised me, reflected in his word choice. Was he nervous?

My chest filled, and I felt lighter than air. "Yeah, I am. The book is the most interesting thing I've encountered in a long time. In fact, I haven't been able to stop thinking about it." His uncertainty, his obvious fear of rejection, gave me the courage to be more truthful.

His responding smile was shy. "Okay."

I nodded and went to walk away when his fingers tangled in mine. He tugged me toward him. My skin tingled from the sensation of our hands intertwined.

"I'll see you later." The words were simple, but there was a heavy intent in them I couldn't help but hear.

He wanted to see me. He liked me. I wasn't crazy, and I wasn't reading into things. Oh my God, I couldn't wait to talk to Joshua about it.

"I'm looking forward to it." I knew he could probably hear the nervous, excited tremble in my words, but I didn't care. I didn't want to hide it from him. I wanted him to see how I felt.

"I'd better go," he said, but our fingers were still locked together.

I crooked the corner of my mouth. "You'll have to let go of my hand first."

He gave me a toothy grin. Released my hand and, with a slow nod, turned and walked away.

I floated through the rest of the day. Classes went by in a hazy blur. My mind was wrapped around the intoxicating memory of Benjamin's fingers holding mine. Out in the hallway, where everyone could see. No mistaking his intent there.

When I got to psych, he was already in his seat. His lips were curved as he watched me walk toward him. My pulse throbbed in my ears, a roar like the ocean.

"Hi," I whispered when I sat down.

"Hi," he whispered back, still staring. Still smiling.

Mrs. Brandwright walked in and closed the door. "Quiz time, folks—this part is multiple choice. I hope you're ready, because it's a doozy. The essay quiz on Friday will be even more fun." Her smile looked downright evil.

Regretfully, I turned my attention away from Benjamin and gave the quiz my best. It didn't help that every five minutes, I kept glancing at the lean lines of his muscled back, the way his arms flexed as he wrote. But I didn't want the teacher to think I was cheating, so I kept those peeks brief.

The final bell rang. At least I made it through most of the quiz.

I got up and gathered my stuff, then dropped my quiz on the desk. I stood outside the door, waiting for Benjamin. Eager to pick our conversation back up. Eager to touch his hand again.

Would he ask me out? Had he talked to Zach and now knew we were just friends? Benjamin would probably wait until after prom, out of courtesy for his cousin. I could be okay with that.

A heavy yank on my arm tugged me away from the door. I whipped around and saw Joshua. "Hey! What are you doing?"

"Did you forget? We're going out. Come on—I want to hit the mall early since I have to study."

Crap. I'd forgotten all about that. I couldn't ditch Joshua to wait for Benjamin. "Okay, okay." I went with him to my locker and grabbed my backpack, filled it with books and notebooks for studying tonight. I hadn't seen Benjamin walk by, but maybe I'd missed him.

Should I text him? Was he looking for me?

To hell with it. I was going to do it. I typed out a brief message and explained I had to take off, ignoring Joshua's foot-to-foot shuffling right behind me, then hit send. Then I let my best friend take my hand and practically yank me out the school doors.

CHAPTER TWENTY-TWO

Joshua

I don't know." Camilla twirled her wrist to study the dozen glinting gold bangles stacked in a row. "Does this look like me? I don't normally wear jewelry like this. It's a little . . . bold."

"I think it's perfect. Gold and red go nicely together." I sipped my soda and peered at the rack. "But I also like this coppery color, which complements your skin tone."

"Oh, that's prettier." She picked up the copper bangle set and slid them on. "Yeah, I dig this more. Perfect. And look, there are even earrings that match!" She grabbed those too and put them in her small wicker basket.

"So did he text you back?" I asked. Camilla had filled me in on what happened with her and Benjamin today. For once, I was glad to be wrong—apparently the guy *had* been trying to send her a secret message. And holding her hand like that in the hallway at school was definitely not the act of a casual friend. "Have you guys talked about hanging out, or are you too shy to ask, given what happened last time?"

She flushed. "I haven't brought it up yet. I'm trying to just live in the moment instead of worrying about where it'll lead. I've realized I spend too much time feeling anxious over things that haven't even happened yet. Worries about prom sucking. Worries about Benjamin not wanting to date me. On and on and on. All of it was wasted energy. So I'm happy texting him and connecting with him right now."

"Fair enough. So what's up with prom? Is he going?"

"We haven't talked about it since our school project, but he'd said back then that he was probably staying home." She tucked a strand of hair behind her ears. "And that's okay. He seems fine with me going with his cousin, and after prom is over, he and I can probably start dating for real. The timing is awkward, but we're gonna roll with it."

"We'll make sure to send him pictures of how beautiful you look."

She gave me a grateful smile in response. "We'll all be looking pretty damn hot, I'm sure."

We moved to the front of the store, where she whipped out some cash and paid for her jewelry. "And I think that's the last of the stuff you needed to get, right?" I asked.

"It is. My mom's gonna be thrilled."

We'd both done some good shopping today. I bought cuff links for my tux and picked up a dress shirt that fit me better than the one I had. Camilla got her jewelry and stockings, plus some hair accessories. She'd even made an appointment at the salon in the mall to get her hair fixed for prom.

After the clerk handed Camilla her small plastic bag, we walked to the mall entrance. Outside, the sun was still shining, even though it was late afternoon. Summer was approaching fast.

"You're sure Zach is okay with me having dinner with you guys? Because I don't want to be a third wheel," I teased.

She shot me a glare. "We already had this discussion. He's perfectly fine with it. And he and I are just friends. Nothing more."

"Okay, okay. I get it." I dug into my pocket and got my car key out, then unlocked the trunk so we could deposit our purchases. "I just wanted to make sure."

We settled in the car, and I pulled out of the parking lot. Camilla dug through my CD collection until she found an old eighties one she liked. When the electronic music came on, she threw her hands in the air and started singing along.

"It's good to see you smiling again," I said. "And I don't just mean about Benjamin, though I'm glad the guy decided to man up and own his feelings. You don't seem so doom and gloom about everything anymore. Why, I think we might actually have fun together at prom."

She snorted. "Thanks, I think. But yes, I think once I realized I was letting all of this drag me into a negative place and I was the only one who could make me feel better, I was able to let it go. It also helps that Zach really isn't as awful as I thought he was. He's kinda growing on me, to admit the truth." She grinned. "Actually, I think you'll like him. He's not a bad guy."

Her phone vibrated, and she pulled it out and smiled at the screen. Instantly, I knew who the message was from.

"What did he write?" I asked.

"'The Beatles or Elvis?'" Her grin was secret and soft, and while I was thrilled about her budding romance, my heart twisted just a touch. Maybe someday I'd have my own Benjamin. Hope springs eternal, right?

"There's only one right answer here. Elvis," I declared loudly to cover up my bittersweet thoughts. "Quick, type fast so he doesn't think there's actually a debate about the issue."

"No way. The Beatles are *far* better. They have a million hit songs, and you can't top their helmet hair. All Elvis had were thrusting hips and a white sequined jumper."

"This might end our friendship," I replied as she typed a response to Benjamin. "There's *no way* the Beatles are better than Elvis. He was smoking hot and had a voice that melted all underwear in a five-mile radius. Watching Elvis do the twist on TV when I was eight was one of my first clues I might be gay."

She barked a laugh. "Okay. I might not agree with you, but I can't argue with your logic."

We made small talk on the way to my house, discussing dinner plans for prom night, when and where we'd meet, and so on. I turned down the street, and as I drove the final block, I realized someone was sitting on my front porch.

Ethan.

Oh my God. My heart rammed against my chest and my breathing grew ragged. I made my hands stay steady on the wheel while I turned the car into the drive. What was he doing here? I stared at his profile, glowing in the setting sun. He had on jeans and a black-and-gray striped shirt, his feet tucked in a pair of brown loafers. His hair danced in the soft late-May breeze.

Casual yet hot, that was Ethan.

"Are we running late or something?" Camilla asked. "Were you supposed to meet him?"

I kept the smile frozen on my face. "No," I whispered out of the corner of my mouth. "I have no idea why he's here."

She squeezed my thigh. "It'll be okay. I'm here for you. We'll get out of the car and be casual. Just three friends relaxing, right? It'll start to feel normal again for you soon enough."

Logically, I knew she was right. The longer he and I practiced being just friends, pretending my confession had never happened, the easier it would get to put it behind us and connect again. But my stupid heart didn't want to do that.

I unclenched the wheel, shut off the engine, and exited. As I made my way to the trunk, I gave Ethan a quick wave.

He nodded in response. "Hey. You guys busy? Should I come back?"

"No, it's fine," Camilla said from behind me as she draped her backpack over her shoulder. "We just went shopping for—" She stopped and gave an awkward laugh. "For relaxing."

Nice cover. From behind the open trunk I shot her a glare, and she shrugged her shoulders in a "Sorry, I panicked" gesture.

I grabbed my bags and closed the trunk. It was so hard to keep my gait natural as I made my way to the front door. Luckily, Camilla was there by my side. I would get through this. I would do this.

"How are you?" I asked, proud of the way my voice was casual. This close, I could see that Ethan's eyes bore a hint of tension, and his pose didn't look so effortless. He seemed tense. Crap. My stomach lurched. This wasn't going to be good.

"Do you have time to talk?" he asked me.

I drew in a slow breath to steady myself before I answered.

Camilla took my bags. "I'll run these inside, Joshua. If you want."

I gave her a nod that it was okay, and she slipped into the house and closed the door behind her. When she left, I straightened and stared at him. His eyes glowed from the sunlight, and I found myself unable to look away. "What's up?"

God, I hoped he wasn't here to tell me we couldn't be friends anymore. That might just about kill me. I already missed him so badly my chest ached. I was torn between relief for getting my feelings out there and regret for how it made our friendship change so drastically.

Ethan licked his lips, and it was so hard to fight the urge to glance down at them. "I didn't ask Noah to prom."

Okay. Not what I was expecting. Then full understanding sank in. "Oh." Guilt hit me swift in the solar plexus. Had my confession ruined his juju that day, and was he still angry with me about it? "Shit. I'm sorry, Ethan. I messed everything up for you." I drew in a breath through my nose and looked down at my shoes.

"You didn't mess it up. I mean, you definitely impacted it." His breathing was as raspy as mine. "But I realized Noah wasn't the right guy for me. So I couldn't do it. I didn't *want* to do it."

I crammed my hands in my jeans pockets because they began to shake. "Why not?" I asked him quietly. My heart gave an irregular beat when his fingers reached out and brushed my arm.

"Since your . . . since you told me how you felt, I've spent my days walking around in a haze. I was a bit angry at first—you'd left me out of a big secret. It made me revisit memories, wondering how I missed the signs. But the anger faded fast, and then I was mortified."

The air locked in my chest.

"No. Shit. I'm messing this up." Ethan sounded frantic. "Please, look at me. I'm so nervous I can barely speak."

I did so. "Are you dumping me as a friend?" I asked him flat out. "Is this your breakup speech or something?"

The shock on his face was genuine. "What? No! No, you're not understanding me. I was mortified because you'd given me a gift in your honesty, and I'd rejected you so coldly. I was angry at myself and stayed away at first because I couldn't stop beating myself up over how I handled it. And then I stayed away because of my conflicted emotions—could you and I really date? What would it be like? Could I even think of you as more than a friend?"

He paused, blew out a deep breath. His fingers shook hard as he reached over and brushed my forearm again. The hairs on my skin shivered from his touch.

"Joshua, you're the best friend I ever had. You've been there for me for so long I don't know how to live without you. And I don't want to. Yes, you shocked the hell out of me, but once your words stuck in my head . . . they were all I could think about. I even realized I'd been jealous over that mall guy."

I stared dumbly at him, unable to believe what I was hearing. My heart throbbed in response.

"I couldn't ask Noah to prom, because I couldn't get you off my mind. Eventually, I figured out that I didn't *want* to stop thinking about you. And even if this is a risk, it's one worth taking." Ethan dropped to one knee and cupped my fingers in his hand. "I hope it's not too late. I'm an idiot who took a long time to realize how he felt and what he wanted. But, Joshua, I want *you*. I want to be with you. I want to date you." He paused, and the emotion in his eyes nearly knocked me off my feet. I couldn't breathe. "I know you probably already have prom plans, because I was the dork who waited so long. And I know this isn't fancy or romantic. I don't have any music or pictures or flowers. But what I'm saying is from the heart. It's real. And if you can save me a dance at prom, I'd be honored. I'm going by myself, and I'd really like to see you there."

"I'm going by myself too," I managed to get out. I lifted him off his knee and took a step closer to him. Only a couple of inches separated our bodies. "So maybe we can go alone together."

"Or maybe we could just . . . go together." His head moved a fraction toward mine. "If you want to."

Every nerve ending in my skin was on fire. My breath came out in soft, eager pants. I nodded. "I'd love to go to prom with you, Ethan."

When his soft lips pressed against mine, I couldn't stop the small sound that escaped my mouth. Ethan wrapped his arms around me, drew me into the warm embrace of his firm body. I let my hands roam his back and kissed him deeply, with all my soul. He tasted of mint and male, and his tongue swept my mouth in a heady rush.

A loud squeal came from the doorway, and Ethan and I broke apart with a laugh. We turned and saw Camilla clapping, tears running down her face.

"Oh my God. It's about time," she said as she sniffle-laughed. "I couldn't be happier for you guys."

Ethan's hand slipped down and his fingers wove with mine. I could see the erratic pulse at the base of his throat. That kiss had impacted him too.

He brushed another soft kiss across my lips. "Let's go inside. We have some prom planning to do."

CHAPTER TWENTY-THREE

Camilla

"Dinner. Was. Perfect," I declared as I patted my stomach. I shot Zach a thankful smile. "You didn't have to buy my food, you know."

"I know. But it seemed like the gentlemanly thing to do." His responding smile was wide and generous.

"I appreciate it." I had to admit, Zach had been a perfect gentleman all evening so far. After picking me up and taking a billion pictures with my family, he'd had the limo driver swing by and pick Ethan and Joshua up, too. The four of us went to a nice steak house on the West Side. Conversation had been easy and peppered with laughs.

Zach held the door open for me, Joshua, and Ethan to exit the restaurant. All of us were groaning a little because of how much we'd eaten. At least my formfitting red dress was made of stretchy fabric.

We got in the limo and rode toward the hotel hosting our prom night. I couldn't wait to see it all decked out, to see how dressed up everyone got.

"You look amazing, by the way," Zach said to me for the fifth time since he'd picked me up. "You sure you want to just be friends?" He gave an exaggerated waggle of his eyebrows. "'Cause you're gonna miss out on all of *this*." He waved a broad hand over his tux.

I barked a laugh. "I do have to admit, you're looking pretty foxy."

"I'll say." Joshua gave Zach an intense stare and eyed him up and down, and Zach blushed, which made all of us laugh harder. Ethan elbowed Joshua in the side, and he fake wheezed.

I snuck my phone out and shot Benjamin a quick text. *Hey, I'll send you a msg tonight when I get home. Hope your evening is good. I'll miss you!* I'd made a promise to myself that I wouldn't spend all night on my phone, waiting for texts from him. Zach deserved better than that. But it didn't mean Benjamin wouldn't be on my mind.

Finally, the limo pulled into the parking lot. I squirmed in excitement in my seat.

"We're here, bitches!" Joshua proclaimed. "Time to party!" He pushed the door open and let all of us out.

Zach pulled me over to the side, and we separated from Joshua and Ethan. "I just wanted to tell you, before we head in, that I've had a great time so far."

"Me too." I squeezed his upper arm. "I mean, I know we got off to a rocky start, but I'm glad I'm here with you."

His cheeks burned. "Really?"

"Absolutely. And I hope that after graduation we keep in touch. You're a nice guy, Zach."

He gave me a big hug. "I know I keep telling you this, but you look beautiful," he whispered in my ear.

His praise filled me with warmth. I'd had my hair styled at the salon, including freshening up my colored streak with a bold flash of red, and I was decked out in my strapless red dress with the inappropriately high slit up the right thigh. I felt sexy and pretty and daring today. "You're a knockout too."

As we headed toward the hotel entrance, I saw a group of fellow seniors standing to the side. A slender brunette named Brianna was eyeing Zach so hard, I was pretty sure her eyes were going to fall out.

"Hey," I whispered. "I sense some vibes coming your way from Brianna. No, don't look," I rushed to say. "Play it cool."

Fortunately, Zach took my advice and didn't gawk at her. Maybe he was learning after all. "No way. I know who she is—she's that gorgeous girl in my art class. Way out of my league. What should I do?"

"When we get inside, offer to get her a drink and tell her how gorgeous she looks."

"You make it sound so easy."

"It is." I rolled my eyes. "Just be a gentleman and don't come on too fast. From the look she was giving you, I think she'd be interested in a dance or two."

The lobby was filled with dolled-up seniors strolling around in their finest formal wear, talking loudly and laughing. Music thumped from the large ballroom off to the left. I sighed as a little flash of sadness swept over me.

Zach stopped me in the middle of the lobby. "I have a confession to make."

"What's that?"

He peered over my shoulder and gave a nod. "I asked someone

to come. I'm going inside, so meet me in there soon, okay?"

"What are you talking about?"

His smile was bittersweet as he hugged me again, then thrust my prom ticket into my hand. "See you inside." Then he walked off toward the ballroom.

Okay. Did he just ditch me before we even got inside? What was going on here?

A low whistle came from just a few inches behind me, and an achingly familiar voice said, "Wow."

My heart was threatening to slam its way out of my chest as I turned around and faced Benjamin. "But . . . What . . . ? I thought . . ."

"Surprise." His smile was wide and lit me up from the inside out. He reached for my hand and kissed the top. "You look stunning. I've never seen anyone so beautiful."

I flushed from head to toe. Benjamin looked like he'd been poured into his tux. It fit him like a second skin. "I don't understand. I thought you weren't coming."

His fingers wrapped around my bare upper arm and seared me with the heat coming off him. I'd never seen his eyes so intense, so fixed on me before. "I borrowed the tux from my brother. Zach told me when you guys would be here. He heavily recommended I come. So I bought my ticket last-minute."

Tears burned the backs of my eyes. I blinked rapidly. I owed Zach another big hug. "That was really generous of him."

Benjamin stepped to me so our chests touched. His scent wrapped around me, filled me. I closed my eyes and just breathed. Just lived. He took me in his arms and pressed a soft kiss to my jaw, and little shivers danced across my skin there. "For so long I fought my feelings because I knew Zach had it bad for you. But he and I talked, and I think he's cool with us dating."

"I'm so glad."

The rest of the world faded away as his eyes grew hooded and he leaned down to take my lips in a kiss. God, I'd been waiting ages to feel it again, and it was just as breathtaking as I remembered. His mouth moved expertly over mine, teasing and nipping. I heard a couple of whistles around us but chose to ignore them. Wrapped my arms around him and hung on to his shoulders for dear life.

When we finally pulled away, his eyes were a bit hazy—no doubt they matched mine. "Be my girlfriend," he asked me.

I nodded, smiled. Gave him another soul-searing kiss, although this one was quicker.

We pulled apart and held hands, just standing in the lobby for a moment. Enjoying the fuss and craziness around us. My smile was so wide I knew I looked ridiculous, but I didn't care at all.

Through the hotel's double doors I saw Karen come in, wearing a slim black dress and black heels. To her left was her friend Monica. The two girls chatted as they made their way in. I was glad to see her come to prom, even if it hadn't worked out the way she'd hoped.

She stumbled a moment when her eyes locked on David and Ashley, who stood off to the side, holding hands and talking rapid-fire with another couple. I saw Karen straighten her back and lift her chin. She whispered something to her friend, then walked over in a confident stroll to David and Ashley.

David tensed immediately. Uh-oh.

"Hey, one of my friends is waving me over," Benjamin told me as he squeezed my fingers. "I hadn't told anyone I was coming, so he's probably surprised. I'm gonna ask where he's planning to sit.

You wanna come with me or hang here? I'll just be a minute."

"I'll stay here, if you don't mind." To be honest, I wanted to see what was going to happen with Karen. Had she taken my advice and was she going to make amends? I hoped so. Senior year was almost over.

Benjamin left to talk to his friend, and I tried to absorb myself into the wall and pretend like I wasn't being nosy. I saw Karen and David lean toward each other. Ashley stood there in silence, her face showing an array of emotions.

Then Karen reached over and gave David a quick hug, and he smiled at her. My heart melted at the sight. *Yay!* I cheered on the inside. When I saw Karen and Ashley hug too, then wipe at their mascara, I did a little quiet clap. Monica joined their group, and all of them walked into the ballroom together.

Benjamin came back and took my hand again. The heat from his palm seeped into mine. "I peeked into the ballroom. It looks super crowded. Almost elbow to elbow."

Part of me was excited to enter and start dancing, but the other part wanted to linger for another moment alone with Benjamin. Well, relatively alone. I kept stealing glances at him as we stood side by side.

Boyfriend. He was my boyfriend. I couldn't believe it.

"I'm really glad you finally read *Cyrano*," he said, and I saw a flicker of vulnerability in his eyes. "I was going to feel really dumb if you didn't. Or if you did but had decided you didn't like me any-more. Or didn't understand the message I was trying to send you."

I squeezed his hand and rubbed my thumb along his skin. "I can't believe it took me that long to remember the play title. I feel like an ass."

"I didn't exactly make it easy on you. I was torn because I liked you, but I couldn't do anything about it." His eyes met mine, and we both smiled.

Then I heard a slurping sound behind us, and we both looked at the source. Against the corner of the wall was Niecey, pinned by Dwayne, practically making a baby.

I gave an awkward laugh. "We should get out of here."

"Yeah. There's no way a teacher isn't going to bust them."

We moved toward the ballroom, and my heart rate picked up in excitement. I squeezed his hand.

"I hope you save me a dance," he said in a light tone as we crossed the threshold.

I shot him a sly smile. "If you're nice enough tonight, I'll save you two."

CHAPTER TWENTY-FOUR

Joshua

I watched Camilla enter the ballroom with Benjamin. The two of them made such a striking couple. She'd outdone herself tonight and was more beautiful than I'd ever seen her, and Benjamin looked seriously hot in his formfitting tux. And I wasn't the only one who had noticed. I didn't think Camilla had stopped smiling since she'd seen him in here—well, except for a small break for that PDA kissing display. Downright scandalous.

Ethan nudged me on the upper arm. "How do you feel about that?" he asked, nodding in her direction.

"Glad, actually. Though it took me a while to get on board with it. I admit, that hot-and-cold thing he was doing made me mad because I saw how crushed she was. And when they started talking again, I was afraid at first that he'd hurt her by leading her on, but I really do think he cares about her."

"I agree." Then Ethan cleared his throat and his cheeks burned, and my heart flipped in response. God, he was so damn cute. "So . . . you don't think this"—he waved at the air between both of us—"is weird in any way, right?"

I paused and really made myself consider it. Dinner tonight had been fun and entertaining. We'd all talked like we used to, no stress, no pressure. Just hanging out and relaxing and cracking jokes and stuffing our faces with fine cuisine. On the limo ride over, yeah, I'd been super aware of Ethan's body beside mine. But that wasn't anything new. I'd carried those feelings for years.

No, the newness came with that heated look in his eyes I'd never seen before Tuesday night. The one that said Ethan finally noticed me as more than a friend, a look I never thought I'd see. He really was attracted to me. More than once tonight I'd caught him eyeing me when he thought I wasn't paying attention. Which meant I'd been walking around for the last couple of hours with a warm, glowing feeling inside me.

I wanted to burst with happiness.

"Weird? Not one bit," I answered. I leaned close to him. Let him see the full intensity of my feelings. "Do you?"

He shook his head. His eyes grew darker, and he whispered, "I want to kiss you again."

Since the promposal three nights ago, he and I had been spending a lot of time together—as friends, as more. Studying for finals, watching movies with Camilla, even hanging with my dad, who'd been happy to see us dating. My feelings for Ethan just continued to grow with every hand-holding, every kiss we shared. "I want to kiss you again too. But we don't want to be like *them*." I chuckled as I nodded in Niecey and Dwayne's direction.

Like she'd been beckoned, one of the history teachers came storming through the crowd and tapped Dwayne on the shoulder. His mouth released Niecey's with a pop, and several people around us giggled. The teacher wagged her fingers at them and told them how inappropriate it was to basically dry-hump in the fancy hotel lobby, and they dutifully nodded at her chastising, then went into the ballroom. Where I figured they'd found a dark corner to continue.

Ethan's pinky finger slid along the outside of my hand. The feel of him reaching out to touch me would never get old.

"I can't believe we're here, together," I whispered. My throat tightened with unexpected emotion. I loved this guy so much, and everything I'd hoped for was coming true. Finally.

Ethan glanced around, then brushed the softest of kisses across my lips. When he leaned away, his smile was intimate and made my stomach flutter. "I'm glad we are. This is exactly where I want to be."

We walked to the ballroom and handed the lady manning the table our tickets. She eyed us oddly at first, probably since there was no girl with us. Ethan clutched my hand and stared her down. When she realized we were a couple, her eyes grew wide and filled with emotion.

"You two look awesome," she said with a wink. "Have a blast in there. And don't spike the punch, boys. The administrators will be watching for that."

I snorted, and Ethan pressed his hand to my lower back and led me into the room. His fingers seared me clear through my jacket and shirt, and I leaned back against the thrilling sensation. We found the table where Zach, Camilla, and Benjamin sat, sipping out of clear plastic goblets and talking among themselves.

"Hey," Camilla said as she beamed at the two of us with pleasure. "About time you two lovebirds made it. We wondered if you were ever going to come inside."

"We were too busy watching Dwayne and Niecey get busted in the lobby," I told her with a laugh.

"Saw them earlier. I figured it would happen," she replied, shaking her head.

Ethan helped me out of my jacket—yeah, I did swoon a little at that gentlemanly gesture—then slid his off and draped them across our chairs. "I'm going to get us something to drink. Wait right here."

Like I would go anywhere.

Apparently, he read the smart-assed look on my face, because he chuckled. "Right. Okay, be back in a minute."

I sat down and let the table conversation wash over me. The room was full to capacity. I was pretty sure almost every senior was in attendance. How cool. On the edge of the dance floor I saw Madison and Tyler suctioned together at the lips. I couldn't help but laugh—at least everything was going okay for them now. Seemed like she'd forgiven him for good.

A few minutes passed as I waited, then another few. What was taking Ethan so long? I stood and looked around the room . . . and saw him talking to Noah.

My heart lurched for a moment, and it was hard to remind myself that he was with me now, that he didn't like Noah anymore. Well, I hoped. I stood and watched them in what I prayed looked like a totally confident stance. Both guys were beautiful and lean and so, so very hot. The impulse to move to Ethan's side was too much to resist, so I made my way over.

When Ethan saw me approach, his smile grew wider and he waved at me. I stopped really close to his side and heard him give a low chuckle. Apparently, my tiny, little, insignificant bout of jealousy was more obvious than I wanted it to be.

"Noah was just telling me about the guy he came to prom with," Ethan said smoothly to me.

Noah beamed, and I could see his molars glinting in the flashing colored lights. "His name is Filip, and he just moved to the United States from Sweden. He barely speaks English, though I've been tutoring him for a couple of months now. He's sitting over there." He gave a jaunty wave.

I peeked over. There was a totally ripped pale-blond guy almost bursting out of his dress shirt at a distant table, waving back to Noah and wearing a shy grin on his face. I gave the guy a courtesy nod, then turned my attention to Ethan and Noah. "He seems . . . nice." And a total beefcake. No wonder Noah was hot for him.

Noah and Ethan chitchatted for another moment, and then Ethan and I walked back to our table.

Let it go. Let it go, I ordered myself. But my stupid mouth didn't seem to hear my brain. "Noah was dressed up very nicely." To say the least. I had yet to see the guy wear something that didn't make him look like a movie star.

"Yeah," Ethan said in a noncommittal tone. "He was."

"And his date was very handsome."

"Mm-hmm." He tugged me a touch closer to his side, and a girl I hadn't seen ran right by me, yelling an apology as she plowed through the crowd in a fiery orange sequined dress.

I was like a dog with a bone. Couldn't drop the subject. "Those two make one good-looking couple."

Ethan stopped a few feet from our table and eyed me. "Are you worried about Noah? I'm picking up some subtle vibes from you." His eyebrow quirked.

Gee, what gave it away? My neurotic pressing, maybe? I sighed. "Sorry. I know how you felt about him, and . . . I'm a little insecure," I made myself finish.

Ethan took my cup and placed it on the table along with his, then straightened and faced me. He drew both of my hands into his. "Joshua. Yes, I had a crush on Noah. I can't hide it or pretend like I didn't."

"I know." A wave of embarrassment hit me, and I sat silent for a moment. God, this love stuff was making me so unsettled and nervous. So afraid of messing up and maybe driving him back to Noah. Music hummed and bounced between the two of us. "Sorry. I feel like an idiot for even being upset still. I know it's not fair."

"Don't apologize." The lights bounced off Ethan's hair and made his skin glow. His thumbs stroked my skin and sent ripples of pleasure across my flesh. I bit back a longing sigh. "I figured out that my crush on Noah wasn't reality. I liked him because he's attractive and he seems like the perfect guy on the surface. But I didn't know Noah at all beyond those things. Not like I know you."

I squeezed his hands and nodded. Okay, I got that.

He kept staring into my eyes. "While you and I weren't talking, I realized something big. The fantasy of Noah can't compare to the reality of Joshua."

His words blew me away. I inched closer until only a sliver of air separated us. "I love you," I whispered.

"I'm falling for you too," he whispered back. "How could I not? You're perfect—for me."

Everything, every ounce of love I felt, rushed to the surface, and I knew I'd found my happiness.

The music changed to a slow song. Ethan gave me a smile that spread over me like warm honey. "Let's dance, shall we?"

I nodded, unable to fight my own broad grin. "Lead the way."

Here's a proposal you can't refuse.

FLIRT

PORTRAIT OF US

A. DESTINY and RHONDA HELMS

The small old woman stared hard at the croissants. She tapped her wrinkled lips with a pudgy hand. "I can't decide if I want three or four," she mused.

I smiled and dusted my flour-coated hands on my jeans. "Take your time, Miss Figler. I'm right over here if you need anything." I stepped a few feet to the left and kneaded the pizza dough a little more, getting it to just the right texture.

"Corinne?" she asked. "I think I'll have four. And a couple of your grandfather's scones. They're the best I've had since I visited England."

"Grandpa loved London," I told her. "I think he studied under a baker while he was there." I prepared her order and boxed them, then rang her up. Then I divided the pizza dough into separate bags and popped them in the freezer.

Saturday mornings were either super slow or super busy. Right now we were having a slow stretch. But it gave me time to get caught up on packaging call-in orders, make more dough, and clean up my station.

The only downside was, I wasn't quite distracted enough to keep my mind off my art project. In yesterday's class, I'd turned in my entry. I'd stayed up late every night this week working on getting it just perfect. Long after my family had turned in, I'd hovered around my easel, washing layer after layer of watercolor over the image.

When I'd put the last touches on it on Thursday night, I'd collapsed in exhaustion in bed and nearly overslept yesterday morning.

Almost every student in class had turned in a piece for the competition. My stomach had been in knots. A few students in there I'd anticipated, sure—but I hadn't expected that many people. The weekend was going to drag painfully slowly, especially if we didn't get more customers in.

My grandfather popped his head out and gave me a wink. His dark golden eyes glinted in the bakery's lights. "Everything okay out here?"

I grabbed the bleach and began scrubbing down the counters. Grandpa ran a tight ship, and he insisted on the place being clean. *A sloppy shop turns customers off,* he always preached to me.

"Things are fine," I replied. "It's a little slow but not horribly so."

Grandpa stepped out and surveyed my progress. He nodded. "Doing a good job. Keep up the hard work."

I warmed under his praise. He was a tough boss, one who

pushed me to do better. If I was giving a 100 percent, he wanted a hundred and ten. But this job had taught me a lot so far. Plus, having extra money in my pocket—that I'd earned myself—was never a bad thing.

"How's things at home?" he asked as he walked to the bread shelf and straightened the loaves.

"Good. Mom asked if you wanted to come over for dinner tomorrow, by the way," I said.

His nod was short. "Can do."

Grandma had passed away a few years ago, from cancer. He'd loved her heart and soul, and though he wasn't one to show a lot of emotion, her death had broken his heart. We'd all been worried that Grandpa would pull away, so Mom had started insisting he come over for Sunday dinner from time to time. That, plus the business, had spurred Grandpa to get out of bed every morning.

Time hadn't erased all the pain, but he was gradually getting his old self back. Mom, however, hadn't backed off on having him over regularly. But it was nice having him around.

The phone rang. He shuffled back into his office, and I heard his gruff voice as he took someone's order. Not the most emotional man, but his cakes were out of this world. And his designs . . . I didn't know how he did it. He'd never gone to art school, yet somehow they were richly decorated, sheer perfection.

While I added a few more croissants to the glass case in front of our counter, the door dinged. In walked Matthew, followed by a few of his basketball-jock friends. The guys behind him were loud, shoving each other, and I fought the urge to roll my eyes.

I had to be nice to the customers, even if they were super annoying.

Or if one of them had piercing blue eyes that kept drawing my attention back.

I was glad Grandpa wasn't here to see the hot flush on my cheeks. He was pretty astute and would see it immediately. I cleared my throat. "Can I help you?"

One of Matthew's friends, a stocky Asian who I think was going to be a senior this year, pursed his lips. He strolled to the counter, dragging his fingertips along the glass. Ugh. "I want a doughnut," he said, looking back at his two buddies.

Matthew's brow furrowed, and he bore holes into his friend's face. What was that all about?

The guy cleared his throat, then glanced back at me. "Uh, please."

At least one of them had manners—and enough common sense to make the other ones behave politely. Guess I could give Matthew a point of credit for that one. I gave a nod and walked over to the doughnut section. "What would you like?"

The guy tilted his head. His black hair was spiked in the front, and he rubbed a hand absently over the top of it. "Something loaded with chocolate."

Matthew's other friend, a guy who was in science with me this year—Thomas—came to the counter too. "Hey, get two of them. You owe me for buying you a Coke yesterday."

The first guy grumbled, then nodded.

I pulled two chocolate-covered doughnuts out and made myself look at Matthew. For some stupid reason, my pulse picked up. "Anything for you?" At least my tone was steady, even if a little chilly.

He shook his head and pursed his lips. "I'm not sure yet."

I put the doughnuts in individual minibags and rang the two guys out. They clomped to the door.

"Hey, man, you coming?" Thomas asked as he shoved his shoulder to the door. The little bell rang, and a blast of warm air burst inside.

"I'll be out in a minute," Matthew replied.

The guys shrugged, then started chowing on their doughnuts as they headed outside into the warm summer heat.

Matthew took his attention off the glass case, then gave me a crooked smile. "Sorry about them. I don't think they get enough oxygen in their brains."

That made me crack a small smile. At least he felt bad for them being such meatheads. "Anything in there interest you?"

He tilted his head, and a smile widened on his face.

"Um, what?"

"You have . . ." He reached toward me, then stopped, gesturing at my cheek. "Uh, there's a little flour . . ."

Ah, crud. I spun around and scrubbed at my cheeks. When I kneaded dough, flour got everywhere. Why hadn't I thought it would be on my face, too? Awkward. I turned back and fought the wave of embarrassment. "Thanks."

Matthew leaned toward the case, careful not to touch the glass and keep his fingers on the metal rim. "So, how did your project come along? You entered, right? I thought I saw that."

I swallowed. Somehow I hadn't anticipated him asking me about art. But of course he would. "It went fine, thanks." My spine was so stiff I could snap in half if another breeze rolled in here. What was it about him that set me on edge so much? "So . . . you entered?" I made myself ask.

"I did. Took me all week to work on my piece. I stayed up really late."

I tried to envision what postmodern art he would have

worked on that could take more than ten minutes. Then I shoved that snotty thought out. Ava's words about me being judgmental popped to the forefront of my brain. "I did too, actually. I did a watercolor for my entry."

"I did an ink-and-newspaper collage for mine. Kind of a mixed media. A bit of a social commentary . . ." He gave a self-conscious shrug, then cleared his throat. "Um. Anyway. Good luck. I've seen your pieces, and you're really talented."

Wow, that was really nice of him. My heart thudded in surprise at the compliment. If Ava were here, she'd be poking me in the ribs. "Thanks. I appreciate that. And good luck to you, too."

Matthew rubbed a hand over the back of his neck. His Adam's apple bobbed as he swallowed, and I couldn't tear my gaze away. As much as I hated to admit it, he really was handsome.

"I'll see you Monday, then," he said, his grin crooked as he backed away from the counter.

I tipped my head in response and watched him turn to leave. Every movement of his was effortless, from the way his legs ate up the distance between him and the door to how his arm reached out and pushed it open. A sort of ballet, full of confidence and self-assurance.

Wow, was I getting ridiculous or what? Maybe I'd breathed too much flour in this morning. I shook those thoughts out of my head and turned my attention back to cleaning. *Focus,* I ordered myself. A guy could be as cute as he wanted, but that didn't mean he thought I was cute in return. Or that I'd even want him to.

I had enough on my plate. There was no room in there for a guy.

Especially one like Matthew.

About the Author

RHONDA HELMS is the author of *Struck* (as Rhonda Stapleton), plus several Flirt novels with Simon Pulse. She lives in Northeast Ohio with her husband, two kids, and a crazy dog and cat. To learn more about Rhonda, visit her website at rhondahelmsbooks.com.